peter
Darling

Peter Darling
By Austin Chant

Published by Less Than Three Press LLC

Edited by Amanda Jean and James Loke
Cover designed by Natasha Snow

First Edition February 2017
Copyright © 2017 by Austin Chant
Printed in the United States of America

Digital ISBN 9781620049587
Print ISBN 9781620049808

This book is for every villain who ever inspired a queer awakening, and for every queer child who ever saw a piece of themself in the enemy.

It's also for Simone, who is definitely a villain of some kind.

Acknowledgments

This book would not exist without the incredible work and dedication of my editors. James: Thank you for seeing the heart of this book and for so frequently guiding me back to it—and for sending approximately one million passive-aggressive text messages to make sure I kept working. Amanda: Thank you for grounding and wrangling me, and also, you were right to make me take out the nonessential descriptions of Hook's outfits (may they rest in peace). You both have my eternal thanks for fielding my late-night panic texts, disruptive flashes of inspiration, and existential despair. I adore you!

Other people who saved my ass: my beta team, a.k.a. Simone, Keezy, and Cora. Thank you for your emotional support and killer feedback, and for challenging me to do better. You're the coolest.

peter

Darling

Austin Chant

"Each new truth destroys the one held before it."
- Magnus Hirschfeld

Prologue

James Hook was bored.

The woods had grown rather tame, he thought. Time was, he and his pirates would have been fending off tigers, wolves, and little boys with swords; they would have been snarled in thorns and clinging vines, beset by swarming fae, ambushed by roving crocodiles. Nowadays, though Neverland was still overgrown, it was no more threatening than an unkempt lawn.

It was the morning after a powerful rain, but the sun was shining, and dew gathered like jewels on the leaves. From where Hook was reclining, in the velvet cushions of a sedan chair carried by four straining men, the forest had a fresh polish and smelled like the coming of autumn.

There were even sweet little birds singing. It was repulsively saccharine.

"Which way at Eagle Pass, Captain?" called Samuel, Hook's bosun since the retirement of old Smee. Samuel was walking ahead, where Hook could admire his arse.

Hook glanced listlessly at the treasure map on his

knee, lifting his lacy cuff so he could see the twist of the path. "East," he said, and the party veered east.

They had liberated the treasure map from One-Eyed Jack, captain of the *Devil's Pride*, after a brief and unsatisfying battle. The *Devil's Pride* was currently sinking to the bottom of the sea, and Hook had sent all of One-Eyed Jack's loyalists off the plank, but it hadn't sated him. He was bloodthirsty, and he had nothing to vent his bloodlust on.

The pirates followed his directions into a tight thicket, where the trees grew close to the narrow path. The sedan chair was almost too wide to fit through, but the men knew better than to suggest that Hook get down and walk. They struggled gamely on until the trail emerged into a wide gulch shaded by birch trees. An enormous log had fallen across this ravine, leaving a shallow space just tall enough for a man to crouch under. And there, beneath the log, was a boulder carved with a particular sign—the sigil with which One-Eyed Jack had signed his letters.

Hook sighed, unable to muster much enthusiasm. "Down," he commanded, and his pallbearers set the sedan chair down to rest on its base. "Roll that boulder aside and start digging."

It would be dirty, sweaty work to squat beneath the log and dig up the fortune of gold and jewels rumored to be buried there. Hook was looking forward to it; the sight of other men toiling usually made him feel better. Samuel, especially, had a way of making sweat and grime look appealing. It would at least soothe Hook's soul, if not solve his boredom, to watch Samuel roll up his sleeves and grasp his shovel with those bulging forearms.

Therefore hopeful, Hook settled in for the show.

Half an hour or so later, he began to think that a book would have made for better entertainment. He could only watch the shovel go up and down so many times, Samuel and the others disappearing behind a growing mound of dirt. The temperature increased as the sun climbed higher; the lesser insects of Neverland grew hungry and agitated as they hovered over the ravine, attracted perhaps by all the sweat. Hook swatted the bugs away with the treasure map, glaring at his men as they dug.

"How much longer?" he demanded.

Samuel stuck his head out of the hole, his brown hair slicked down with sweat. "Hard to say, Captain," he said apologetically. "There's no sign of gold yet."

"Hurry up," Hook said. "If that treasure isn't unearthed within the hour, I'll flog every one of you till I can show you your own spines."

Samuel blanched and ducked back into the hole. Hook sighed, fanning himself.

From behind him someone said: "What's the rush, Captain?"

Hook twisted around in his chair, startled.

He hadn't heard the stranger approach, yet there he was, sitting on a rock at the edge of the ravine. The young man wore baggy clothes and carried no obvious weapons, which was unusual for Neverland.

"Well, hello," Hook said. The stranger was quite handsome, in a lanky sort of way—his face was bony and angular, his limbs narrow and long. His hair was curly, and as raggedy as if it had been hacked off with a knife. "What have we here?"

The stranger leaned forward. "You don't remember me?"

There *was* something familiar about this young

man's coloring and his clear, arrogant voice. "Now that you mention it, I do believe we've met. Where?"

"Here," the stranger said. "In Neverland." He rose, swaying slightly. Hook watched as he picked his way down the ravine. He carried himself like he was half air, as though a mere breeze could lift him off his feet. At the same time, something about his movements raised the hair on the back of Hook's neck. They were not just familiar—they were the footsteps of a cat slinking casually toward a wounded bird.

"Who are you?" Hook asked, curling his fingers around the hilt of his sword.

The stranger paused and gave a slow, cold smile. "I'm the prince of runaways," he said. "The rightful king of Neverland."

"What the hell does that mean?" Samuel shouted. "Tell the captain who you are!"

"Be quiet," Hook snapped without turning his head. He stepped down from the sedan chair, walking to meet the stranger as he descended into the ravine.

The nearer he went, the more handsome the stranger became. His eyes were clever, green, and restless, constantly darting about to take in his surroundings; his mouth was a whimsical line. Recognition tugged again at the back of Hook's mind, but he couldn't place this man anywhere in his memories, and he thought he would've kept a record of that smile.

"Samuel is right. I didn't ask for a riddle." Hook paused at a safe distance. "I certainly didn't ask for arrogant claims. I asked who you are."

"You first," the stranger said.

His entitlement pricked at Hook's nerves, but it also intrigued him. "As you wish." He gave a slight, elegant bow. "I am James Hook, captain of the *Jolly Roger*, leader of Neverland's dread pirates and terror of the seven seas."

Hook was frustrated, and a little fascinated, when the stranger failed to looked impressed. Hook tried again, taking a step closer, pressing the advantage of his height over the slighter man. "My friend," he said, allowing a touch of venom to creep into the words, "you've stumbled upon the excavation of some extraordinarily valuable treasure. It belonged to the last man who challenged me, and you can guess what became of him. Ordinarily, I wouldn't allow a bystander to live if he crept up on me amid such a dig. But *if* you tell me your name, I'll consider sparing your life."

"You know me," the stranger said, calm like the bare edge of a knife.

Hook's patience was rapidly expiring. "Your *name*, stranger," he growled, "or else—"

He caught a flicker of movement under the stranger's collar. A silver gleam, and then the rustle of wings unfolding as a fairy crawled out onto the man's shoulder. Hook knew her at once.

"Tinker Bell?" he asked, uncomprehending.

Then his eyes traipsed back to the stranger's face, to his callous, boyish grin, and Hook's stomach dropped with sudden revelation.

"*You.*"

Peter Pan grinned at him. "Me."

They were only inches apart. Pan shot out his hand and tore a knife from Hook's belt. Hook recoiled, drawing his sword barely quick enough to divert a stab at his heart. Before he could counter, Pan leapt backward—leapt impossibly high, all the way to the top of the ravine, and stayed floating above the ground with the knife in his grip. Tinker Bell glittered on his shoulder.

Hook squeezed the hilt of his sword, fingers trembling with disbelief. "*Pan*." No wonder he hadn't recognized the man; he had been a boy when last Hook had seen him. It had been a decade at least. All that remained of the child now was the cruelty in Pan's smile.

"I remember you being faster," Pan called down to him. "You must be getting old."

"I remember you being smaller," Hook called back. "Where have you been these many years?"

"Having adventures," Pan said airily. "Traveling the whole sea and sky. And now I've come to win the war with you once and for all."

"Liar." Hook gestured to his men. Without looking, he knew they were arming themselves; he saw Pan watching them. "The last I heard, you were a strange little runaway," Hook continued. "Gone back to be with your *family*."

A sudden cloud passed over Pan's face. "You heard wrong," he said. "I don't even know what a family is."

Hook sneered. "Then correct me. Where have you been?"

"Killing pirates," Pan said. "And I think I'll add one more to my tally."

Hook recognized the flash of vicious intent in Pan's eyes that always gave away his attacks before he struck. That gave him the instant he needed to parry as Pan flew at him, quick as a dart. Pan's knife rang hard off the edge of Hook's sword, and Hook swiped up at Pan with his claw, only managing to catch the hem of one of his trouser legs. Pan kicked him in the chest and knocked Hook's sword aside with a blow to the wrist, sweeping forward and plunging his knife into Hook's ribs.

The short blade didn't make it far past Hook's coat, but it broke skin and scraped across bone before Pan tore it out again. Hook howled in surprise as much as pain, staggering back with a hand clapped over the wound.

"Captain!" Samuel bellowed, and fired his pistol. The bullet went wide, but even so Pan recoiled, flying above them with a wild laugh. The pirates aimed their weapons after him, and he disappeared over the treetops, pursued by gunshots.

"I'll be back for you, Captain!" Hook heard him shout.

Hook sank to the ground, staring at the blood on his fingers. The wound throbbed between his ribs, a slow crimson stain spreading on his shirt. He hardly recognized the sensation. It had been so long since someone had hurt him.

He smiled.

One

"What do you remember?" Tinker Bell asked.

Peter folded his arms behind his head, grinning at her. "What do you mean?"

He was floating above the island, weightless on the wind. Tink perched on his chest, clinging to his shirt buttons. She glared her many eyes at him. "Do you remember flying here?"

"Of course," Peter said easily. He had swum through the ocean of stars, following Tink's directions to the second star on the right. They had burst out into a storm above the island and danced along the clouds together, lightning turning the world black and white in flashes.

"And before that?"

Peter had a vague memory that he had been somewhere unpleasant, but in the long dark passage between worlds, that memory had grown far away and unimportant. "No," he said. "I expect I was doing something interesting."

Tink hummed in agreement, and said no more of it. Peter turned over so he could survey his kingdom, spreading his arms out like a sail. The island was covered in forest, except for the snowy peaks of distant mountains; blue rivers raced through the woods, patrolled by wild beasts. The surrounding sea was a pale and pearlescent green, like absinthe, sunlight glinting on the waves.

There was still blood on the knife Peter had stuck in Hook, droplets of it sliding off the point and flying away into the wind. Peter threw the knife into the air, laughing, and caught it by the blade. Naturally, the first thing he had wanted to do was let Hook know that he wasn't in charge anymore; Tinker Bell had warned him that Hook had been ruling Neverland in his absence. Probably Hook had gotten lazy and comfortable while Peter was gone. That would explain why Peter had gotten the best of him so easily.

Well, Peter would have to wake him up. He had no intention of coming back to Neverland without a good war.

~~*

A portly tree with wide branches had served as the Lost Boys' hideout since Peter had first assembled their company. The tree's roots grew down into a substantial cavern below the earth, which the Lost Boys had further hollowed out and made into their home.

The hideout tree flowered in summer, putting out papery pink blossoms that gave way to autumn fruit. It was the only one of its kind in Neverland, and visible from a distance when one flew above the forest. Peter spotted it almost at once, along with the plume of black smoke rising beside it. "They're always making a mess," Tink said.

"Are they all still alive?" Peter asked, coasting down toward the tree.

"You couldn't get rid of them if you tried," Tink said. "There's hardly any bloodshed when you aren't around."

"Then it's a good thing I'm back," Peter said.

He landed on a branch above the hideout tree. In the clearing around it, a bonfire was blazing, several wild pigs roasting on spits above the flames. All around the fire, young men clustered, talking as they sharpened knives and arrowheads. One was poring over a map.

Peter crowed. As one, the Lost Boys looked up.

There was no doubt in Peter's mind that the Lost Boys would remember him, and one by one they paled with shock and recognition. All except for the young man who had been studying the map, who stood slowly, making his way to the front of the gang. The other Lost Boys parted for him.

Peter had never seen this boy before. He wore a wolf pelt around his waist, but otherwise could have been a farmer's son; he had that honest, hardworking look, with broad shoulders and a stern jaw. He stared up at Peter with measured distrust. "Who are you?" he called.

Peter expected the Lost Boys to inform him, but either his asking had cast doubt in their minds or they wanted to let Peter take the stage himself. "You don't know me?" Peter called back. He jumped out to the end of the branch, which failed to dip beneath his weight. "I'm your captain. I should skewer you for your insolence."

"Peter?" That was Slightly; Peter recognized him at once, a reedy young man with inquisitive eyes and round spectacles. "Is that really you?"

The farmer boy glanced sharply at Slightly, as if he were stepping out of line by addressing Peter.

"Yes, it's me," Peter said. He met each curious gaze in turn with a smirk. "Who was it who led you all to stow aboard the *Jolly Roger* in barrels and surprise the pirates in their sleep? Who first talked to a mermaid? Who brought you to meet the fairy queen?"

"Who cares?" the farmer boy said.

Peter frowned. "What's your name?" he asked.

"Ernest."

"Are you a Lost Boy, Ernest?"

Ernest glared up at him. "I'm their leader."

Several of the boys winced and looked askance at Peter, but no one contradicted Ernest.

Peter laughed and swung down from the tree. He was a little annoyed to find that Ernest stood almost a head taller than him; in olden days, he would have cut Ernest short rather than allow another boy to loom over him. "If you're a Lost Boy, then you should know me."

"I do," Ernest said. "You're Peter Pan. But you've been gone ten years, and I'm their leader now."

"Prove it," Peter said, tossing his knife into the air and catching it.

The clearing grew deathly quiet. Ernest glanced at the knife, then back at Peter's face, his eyes narrowing. "We're in the middle of something important," he said. "I'm about to leave on an expedition. If you want to fight over who's the leader when I get back, you're welcome to wait here."

"As if I'd let you run away."

"Run away?" That cracked Ernest's composure. "I'm not scared of you. You're just a story to me."

"Just a *story*?" Peter grinned. "Tell me if this feels real."

He lunged.

Ernest barely evaded the first swipe of Peter's knife, stumbling back and nearly tripping over his feet.

Peter was pleased to see that his reflexes were quick, at least. There wouldn't be any fun in having a rival if he couldn't fight. The other Lost Boys scattered left and right as he drove forward again. Tinker Bell flew from Peter's shoulder with a squawk of amusement, and then settled in a branch above to watch as Ernest ducked and wove, Peter's blade catching only the air.

"Wait," Ernest shouted. "*Wait*!" He seized Peter's wrist in a grip of iron, fingers squeezing so Peter couldn't wriggle free, and yanked it and the knife high above both their heads. Doing so dragged Peter closer to him, and Ernest glared straight into his eyes. "You care about the Lost Boys, don't you?"

"Of course," Peter said, although in that moment he didn't care about much beyond fighting Ernest.

"Come with me," Ernest said. "I want to show you something."

~~*

A spiraling wooden staircase lead inside the Lost Boys' hideout. Ernest lead the way stiffly; he didn't seem to like turning his back on Peter. The roots of the flowering tree formed the hideout's ceiling, snaking down the walls in a protective dome.

Inside, it smelled faintly sour. Tink made a disgusted sound and crawled under Peter's collar. There were weapons everywhere, and beds tucked into cubbies in the walls, furs and rough straw pillows spilling out onto the floor. One bed was occupied, and Peter recognized its occupant at once by his hair, which was almost the same color as Peter's. "Curly?"

Curly didn't answer. He was shivering and wrapped in several furs despite the warmth of the room, his eyes pressed shut. He had grown as much as the others, but huddled up as he was, he looked like a little boy still. When Peter felt his forehead, he found it cold and damp.

Peter snatched his hand back and wiped it on his trousers, grimacing. "What's wrong with him?"

"He got sick about a week ago," Ernest said. "It's been getting worse and worse. He hasn't been able to speak since yesterday." He placed a hand on Curly's shoulder, rubbing it gently. "We've been trying every cure we know of, but nothing helps. Slightly remembered a story about a flower that only grows on the night of a fairy commune. If you make a tea with it, it can heal any illness." Ernest fixed Peter with a grave look. "I don't know how much time he has left. That's why we're going immediately. The mermaids told me there's a commune up on the mountain tomorrow night, and it'll take all the time we have to get there."

"I could just fly there," Peter said.

Ernest looked startled, and almost disappointed, like Peter had ruined his fun. Then he shook his head, collecting himself. "You wouldn't be able to see it from the air," he said. "They choose short trees for their communes so the canopy hides them."

"It doesn't matter. I could still fly up there faster than you could walk."

Ernest's face pinched. "I'm the leader. It's my responsibility to find the flower."

Peter smirked at him. "So you'll admit that I'm the leader if I find it first?"

"You've never even seen the flower."

"Neither have you."

"*You* disappeared for ten years," Ernest said.

"Who's to say you won't disappear again and leave Curly to die?"

"Who's to say you won't fail to get up the mountain, in which case he'll die anyway?"

Ernest turned red. "I don't care who you think you are," he said through gritted teeth. "I'm going, because I don't trust you. That's final."

"Fine," Peter said. "Come if you want. See if you can make yourself useful." Then, because he was annoyed by the insinuation that he was untrustworthy, he reached over and patted Curly on the shoulder as Ernest had done. "I'll be back soon, and you're not allowed to die while I'm gone."

He turned on his heel and went up the stairs to the surface.

Tink laughed beneath his collar. "What's so funny?" Peter asked.

"You," she said. "Grown up. What a joke."

The Lost Boys were still gathered where Peter and Ernest had left them, looking like children whose parents have been shouting in the other room. Peter scowled at them, and they cowered. It didn't make him feel particularly powerful.

Ernest stepped up to Peter's side and folded his arms. He had added a bow and quiver to his arsenal and looked forbidding. "Change of plans," he said. "The lot of you are staying here and looking out for Curly." He glowered over his shoulder at Peter. "Pan and I are going up the mountain."

~~*

Peter supposed it wasn't such a bad distraction from his real quest. He'd get the flower, fix Curly, and

22

then the Lost Boys would fall in behind him when he resumed his war with Hook. Just like old times.

For a while he skipped over the treetops, Tink on his shoulder, while Ernest struggled through the underbrush. He stepped from branch to branch, hands in his pockets, enjoying his view of Ernest's tribulations.

"Are you all right down there?" he called.

"I'm fine," Ernest replied evenly. Peter had to admit he was making good time for someone limited to the ground, and he had barely broken a sweat so far, despite trekking upward into the foothills. "Weren't you supposed to be the boy who never grew up? You look grown up to me."

Peter didn't have an answer; he was fairly sure he had pretended to be immortal to impress the others, but couldn't admit that. "I decided I'd rather be stronger than stay a boy forever," he lied. "There's some things a man can do that a boy can't."

"Like what?" Ernest asked.

"Like have a real war," he said. "Where things are really dangerous."

"Ugh," Ernest said.

Peter had never imagined that a self-professed leader of the Lost Boys could sound so unenthusiastic about war. "How many pirates have you killed?" he asked.

"None."

"What do you mean, none?"

Ernest squinted up at him. "We've been at peace with the pirates."

"*Peace*?" Peter sneered. In the old days, no Lost Boy would have stomached the thought of a truce with one of their mortal enemies.

"Why not?" Ernest asked. "They don't bother us, and we don't bother them."

"Have you made friends with all the lions and tigers too?"

"Those are beasts. The pirates aren't so different from us. It's easy to negotiate with them." Ernest shrugged. "At least for me. Maybe you couldn't."

"I could if I wanted to."

"You couldn't negotiate a peace with your own left foot," Tinker Bell yawned.

Peter glared at her. "That's because only cowards need to make peace. I'll show you how *I* negotiate with pirates." Peter dropped into the undergrowth beside Ernest, drawing his knife to slash through the bunch of brambles ahead. "Things are going to be different now that I'm back."

"I don't know how the Lost Boys survived with you," Ernest said, shouldering past Peter through the bushes.

"They had *fun* with me."

"We have fun. But we don't kill any *people*."

It had never occurred to Peter to think of the pirates as people. "It's just a game," he said. "Who cares?"

"Whatever it is, I don't like it."

Peter pushed up to walk alongside Ernest. He cut his own swath through the forest, ignoring the fact that they were now leaving a trail twice as large for anyone to follow.

They proceeded in unruly silence for a while. Only Tink seemed content. She plucked a small flower from a passing bush and drank its nectar as they walked.

Ernest stopped suddenly when they reached the base of a mossy cliff and swiveled toward Peter. "Say,

Tink," he said. "The story about the flower is true, isn't it?"

Tink shrugged. "It's true for you," she said, in a mysterious shimmer. "The fae give it the power to heal."

Peter frowned at her. "If it's fairy magic, why can't you heal him?"

"Because I'm old. It takes a lot of magic to save a human life. Do you want me to shrivel up?"

"No," Peter said hastily. "It was just an idea."

"The flower is our only choice, then," Ernest said, craning his neck for a better look at the cliff. "I think this'll be a shortcut, if we can scale it. There's a ledge up there that looks like it connects to the path. Peter, can you fly a rope up there?"

Peter took the end of the sturdy grass rope Ernest handed him. "How would you manage without me?" he asked, and shot up to the ledge.

"I'd go around!" Ernest yelled.

The ledge was covered in slippery, emerald-green moss. It wound along the cliff for quite a distance, sloping upward, creating a path for them. It also extended back into a shallow cavern, the floor of which dropped off after a few meters. There was nowhere to secure the rope, so Peter wrapped it around his own hands a few times before tossing the line to Ernest. "Climb up!"

He wasn't anticipating quite how heavy Ernest was. The first time Ernest placed his weight on the rope, Peter jerked forward, banging his knees on the ledge and barely stopping himself from slipping right off. He peered over the edge to see Ernest sprawled on the ground, glaring up at him. The sight made him grin.

"Idiots," Tink said. She took a tiny pinch of silver dust from her wings and tossed it over the rope. At once it lightened, and Peter could stand again, even supporting Ernest's weight. He stood there watching Ernest climb, reluctantly impressed by the muscles standing out from Ernest's arms as he hauled himself up hand over hand.

"You could've made him fly," Peter said.

Tink scoffed. "I don't need two of you." That, Peter thought, was a good point. He didn't want there to be two of him, either.

"What are you talking about up there?" Ernest called, a genuine thread of anxiety in his deep voice. Peter couldn't help but notice that Ernest was gripping the cliff face in addition to the rope, like he didn't trust Peter to hold it sturdy.

"Nothing," Peter said. "Can you climb any faster? My palms are getting sweaty." He grinned at Ernest, who grimaced and did his best to climb faster. "That was a joke," he added. "I wouldn't drop you unless it was on purpose."

Ernest didn't reply; he grabbed the ledge beside Peter's knee. "Move over," he groused. But when his chin cleared the edge, his gaze snapped to something behind Peter and he went white. "Look out!"

Peter and Tink twisted around as one to see a mountain cat crouched in the mouth of the cave, drawn back on its haunches in preparation to pounce. Peter threw himself sideways off the ledge as the cat sprang for him, its claws scrabbling at the rock. He righted himself in the air and heard Ernest yell.

Ernest had managed to pull himself onto the ledge, but the cat had raked its claws over his back, ripping shirt and skin and pulling his bow and quiver out of alignment. As Peter watched, Ernest landed a kick to the cat's jaw, stunning it long enough for him to scramble away across the ledge. The cat, recovered, crouched to spring again.

"Hey!" Peter shouted, swooping above the ledge. The mountain cat startled, hissing, and turned to follow his movements as he flew around the cliff. The moment he saw its attention start to turn back to Ernest, he sailed in and grabbed it by the tail, throwing all his weight downwards and dragging it off the edge. The cat went screeching and clawing down the cliff. When it hit the ground, it fled limping into the woods.

Peter landed on the ledge. Ernest was still half tangled in his bow and trying to pull it off, wincing, bloody lacerations visible through the gashes in his shirt. When he met Peter's gaze, he gave a helpless, embarrassed laugh.

"Thanks," he said. "You saved me."

"You're welcome," Peter said. He stepped forward to extract Ernest from the bow and quiver. "You did warn me about the cat," he added graciously. "Can you keep going with your back like that?"

"I'll be fine," Ernest said. "Let's get to the top of this ridge. There's supposed to be a stream; we can wash out the cuts there."

Peter nodded and led the way.

~~*

There was a terrific view from the top of the cliff, which they reached after another hour or two of climbing. The ground spread out levelly at the cliff's summit before sloping up into mountainside, making it the perfect place to stop and rest. There were scattered trees for shade and a stream that trickled into a clear, waist-deep pool. Ernest, though he continued to act brave, had started to flag. He sank down by the water's edge, pale and wincing. With Peter's help, he rinsed the shallow gashes on his back. Tinker Bell hovered over them, inspecting the wounds and declaring them free of contamination after a sprinkle of fairy dust.

When they were finished, Ernest dangled his feet in the pool, his bloody shirt folded beside him and trousers rolled up to his knees. Peter sat beside him, running his toes over through the cool water. There was an uncertain but comfortable quiet between them, and Peter enjoyed the silence. It had been a long time since he'd sat with another boy in easy intimacy.

He had a sudden memory of curling up with his brothers in a rowboat made of pillows, blankets, and building blocks, a book of illustrated fairytales open between them. *One more story*, Michael had begged, knowing Peter would always say yes.

The memory came with a twinge of pain, of something irreparably lost. Peter stared down at his blurry reflection in the water stirred by Ernest's feet, and for a second his own face looked unfamiliar.

He blinked and it returned to normal.

"You can bathe if you want," Ernest said. "I won't be jealous, even if I can't soak my back."

"He means you smell," Tink said.

"That's not what I meant!" Ernest protested. "Honest, I'm just trying to be friendly—"

Tink cackled.

Peter pulled off his shirt, mostly intending to swat Tink with it. But then he remembered she was old, and probably less resistant to swatting than she used to be.

Besides, he was immediately preoccupied by the hair scattered across his chest—by the shape of his chest itself, flat and smooth, all the way down to his hips.

He stared at it with a nagging, uncomfortable awareness that this had not always been true.

"Peter?" Ernest asked. "What is it?"

"Nothing," Peter said, but he heard his own voice as if he were someone else listening to it. Had it always been so low? He liked it, the deep resonance in his chest, but at the same time it was unsettling. Different.

New.

"It's all right if you're shy," Ernest said.

Peter shook himself and shot Ernest an angry look. "I'm not shy," he said curtly, and more to prove it than anything else he stripped off the rest of his clothes and slid into the pool. The water was cold in contrast to the warm air, and Peter ducked his head under to scrub himself clean of sweat, salt, and dirt.

He surfaced with water running out of his ears and found Ernest watching him. Tink had retreated to sun herself on a nearby bush, leaving them alone. Reflexively, Peter crossed his arms over his chest.

Ernest smiled. "I get shy too," he said. "The others only get embarrassed when they're swimming in front of the mermaids, but I've always felt odd undressing around anyone, especially men."

Peter frowned and sank back into the water up to his eyes, mulling that over. He could remember a time when, as a child, sharing a bath with his brothers hadn't been strange at all. But something had changed him in the interim. There was no denying he felt uncomfortable now.

Ernest was looking at him again. Peter lifted his

head from water and said, "I'm not shy."

"All right," Ernest said. "Don't tell the others that I am, okay?"

"Who cares?" A few long, clinging strands came loose on Peter's fingers when he raked them through his hair—and he remembered cutting it.

A crawling dread came over him, and he plunged his hands into the water, shaking them until the hair was gone. He didn't want to think, so he twisted toward Ernest and asked the first thing that came to mind. "Where did you come from?"

Ernest blinked. "Before Neverland?" When Peter nodded, he stared up at the foliage above them, an odd look on his face. "I don't think about it much anymore. It was so long ago… and I wasn't very happy."

Peter felt a twist of empathy and stiffened. "Why not?"

"I don't know. I don't remember. I knew… I was different somehow." Ernest's face shuttered. "I had to get away from my family. They kept saying there was something wrong with me. In Neverland, nobody cares about that. You can be free."

"I know what you mean," Peter said without thinking.

Ernest looked as startled as Peter felt. "Do you?"

Peter shrugged, attempting nonchalance. Inwardly, he was disturbed to realize it was true. "No one would let me do what I wanted or be who I wanted before," he found himself saying. "In Neverland, they can't stop me."

"Who's they?" Ernest asked. "Your family?"

"No," Peter said. "I don't have a family." His brothers' faces rose in his mind as he said it, but he forced himself to think of them as strangers.

He swam out of the water, crawling into the dry grass. The sun washed over his back, drying the trails of water that trickled from his soaked hair.

"What about Wendy?" Ernest asked.

The name went through Peter like a knife. "*What* did you say?" he spat, ripping up a handful of grass.

Ernest looked taken aback. "The Lost Boys said you went away to be with Wendy. I'm sorry. Should I not have—" Whatever he saw in Peter's face made him shut up and climb hastily to his feet. "Never mind," he said. "Let's go. We've got plenty of mountain to climb."

Two

They slept on a ledge that night, curled up beside the embers of a fire Ernest had lit. In the morning, Peter woke to the nagging sensation that he had forgotten something, but his stomach distracted him. By the time they had finished foraging for breakfast, his mind was pleasantly clear.

That day, as they made their way up the treacherous slopes, Peter didn't fly at all; he trudged beside Ernest, Tink asleep in his hair. Trees stuck out at reckless angles from the mountainside, blown into wild shapes by past storms. The going was difficult, and Peter developed a grudging respect for Ernest's tenacity. He never wavered, no matter how tired he became. He had shrugged off yesterday's wounds and was in good spirits. He seemed to have decided that he and Peter were friends and was much happier that way.

As evening came on, they reached another rough terrace covered in thick forest. Ernest stopped to consult his map. "We *should* be close." He frowned. "The mermaids said the commune would be over a spiny ridge in a white tree. At least I think so—they mimed it. I haven't seen any white trees. What if we went the wrong way?"

"Wait for nightfall," Tink said. "Keep your eyes open."

"What if the mermaids were wrong? If we're on a

different ridge..." Ernest looked close to wringing his hands. Peter clapped him on the shoulder, and felt Ernest startle and then relax under his touch. "I'm glad you're here," Ernest said. "We'll figure something out. But if we don't get that flower..."

"*Wait*," Tink said.

"I hate waiting," Peter said. He flew aloft and circled over the forest, looking for anything out of place, but was met with only a forbidding canopy of dark pines. The sun was going down, and soon it was hard to distinguish anything. If there were a white tree somewhere in the forest, it was impossible to see.

He was about to take a closer look when he heard Ernest give a shout of alarm.

Peter soared back to the clearing, only to see Ernest struggling in the arms of a pirate who had stuffed a gag into his mouth. Surrounding him was a ring of pirates wielding swords and flaming torches, and in the center of them stood Captain Hook.

"Now, where is our dear friend Peter Pan?" Hook was saying. "Heavens, you can't answer me, can you? No matter. I'm sure he'll turn up."

"Hide in the bushes," Tink said softly. "You can catch him off guard."

Peter barely heard her; seeing Hook had sent a bolt of excitement through him, and he felt electric. "Let him go!" he shouted.

Hook threw his head back to stare up at Peter, the torchlight gleaming off his golden earrings and wide grin. "Right on cue," he said. "Come down from there, Pan. We've taken your man hostage." He aimed his pistol at Ernest, who stopped struggling.

Peter came down on his toes across the clearing from Hook. "Let him go," he repeated loudly. "It's me you want."

"Which is exactly why I demand your surrender for his release," Hook said. "Throw down your weapon and I'll free him. If not, he dies."

"He won't let Ernest go," Tink warned. "He'll keep him as a guarantee in case you try to escape."

"Don't listen to her," Hook said.

Ernest said something that might have been Peter's name into his gag. Peter gave him what he hoped was a reassuring look. "How do I know you'll let him go?" he called.

Hook spread his hands innocently. "You have my word as a gentleman."

"You're no gentleman."

"So says the prince of runaways, scrambling around in the woods with no shoes on."

Peter took a step forward, liking the way Hook's eyes followed him. "Duel me," he said. "The only way I'll surrender is if you beat me in a fair fight."

Hook cocked his pistol. "And if I shoot him?"

Peter bared his teeth. "Then I'll really kill you." He took another step forward, and the rest of the pirates edged backward. "If you can beat me, I'll be your prisoner. You have *my* word. But if you hurt him, I'll fly away, and you'll never catch me."

Hook slowly, thoughtfully caressed the trigger of his pistol. Then he lowered the gun, holstered it, and drew his sword.

"A duel it is," he said. "To the death, or the surrender, whichever comes first. You may wish to step aside, Miss Bell," he added, in the direction of Peter's shoulder. "I would hate to have to skewer both of you."

"No thank you," Tinker Bell said, and left Peter's

shoulder for a tree nearby.

"Keep the other boy restrained," Hook snapped at his pirates. "Kill him if Pan tries to run away."

"I'm no coward," Peter said. He smirked as Hook slunk forward. "On second thought, are you sure you're well enough to fight me? I'd hate to think I had an advantage because I wounded you already."

"I'm more than well enough to deal with you," Hook said with a grin. "Come on, brat. Have at thee."

They lunged for each other almost as one. Peter had to twist aside from a spearing thrust of Hook's blade, spinning to the outside of Hook's sword arm. Hook swung to follow him, offering no opening for Peter to exploit, pushing him back with a flurry of little jabs.

Hook fought gracefully, with practiced form, more fencer than buccaneer. His coat swirled around him with each movement. It was a different one than he'd been wearing that morning, as though he had dressed up for the occasion of chasing Peter across the island—and Peter was distracted by it almost long enough for Hook to run him through. He ducked away at the last moment, and Hook's sword sheared through the side of his shirt instead of his belly.

Peter was beginning to realize a flaw in his plan to duel Hook into submission. Now that Hook was on guard, it was impossible to get close to him with a short blade. No matter how he advanced, Hook repelled him, keeping him at a safe distance.

Hook, too, was aware of it. Despite the sheen of sweat on his face, he looked triumphant as Peter retreated from his sword. "Surrender is still an option, Pan," he said, "should you wish to keep your life *and* your dignity."

"*Never.*"

Hook came for him again, and Peter met the blow recklessly, locking their blades together.

That was when he discovered how strong Hook was. Hook simply threw his weight behind his sword and Peter went flying back, slamming into the trunk of a tree. Hook instantly pressed his advantage. Their blades crossed again, and Hook pinned Peter to the tree, the edge of his sword nearly pressed against Peter's throat. Peter could only just hold his sword away with both hands wrapped around the grip of his dagger, and his arms shook with the effort. If he tried to fly free, Hook could easily disembowel him.

Hook was smiling. He braced his stance, increasing the pressure on their joined blades, and Peter grunted and craned his head back as Hook's sword slipped an inch closer to his neck.

He found himself staring up into Hook's face. Peter had never seen him so close, and the picture wasn't foul, but fascinating; his eyes were forget-me-not blue, his hair a tangle of black ringlets, his mustache curled like the crest of a wave. His breath washed over Peter's cheek, and he smelled warm, like spice and salt.

A strange, hot thrill spread through Peter, from his chest to his toes.

"Do you give up?" Hook purred.

"Never."

Hook's smile deepened. "You've forgotten something," he said, and his free hand—no, his iron claw—pressed beneath Peter's chin. It was almost a gentle touch, except that the point of his claw was so sharp, the lightest scrape across his skin raised the hair on the back of Peter's neck. "Surrender now, Pan. Or die."

"To die," Peter began, "would be an awfully big—"

"Don't start *that* again," Hook said. "Surely you could have come up with something new to say after ten years."

Peter laughed, and somehow Hook was laughing with him.

Behind Hook, there was a flash in the night sky. At first Peter thought the flare was a star detaching itself from the heavens; then it came sailing down toward the clearing, and he knew what it was. Hook saw his expression and twisted around. "What in Hell's name is that?" His claw drifted away from Peter's throat.

Peter lifted his feet to press flat against the tree trunk and kicked off, hurling his whole body behind his dagger and knocking Hook off balance. Hook went to one knee but managed to deflect Peter's blade, and for a moment they circled each other in the clearing. Then a shower of sparks descended around them, flooding the forest with milky light.

The pirates cried out in alarm as the fae surrounded them. Two fairies hovered between Peter and Hook. One was Tinker Bell; Peter hadn't even realized she had gone. The other was the fairy queen.

Peter recognized her at once, even though she had aged greatly over the years. She was like a dragonfly, her carapace an iridescent sunset gold, her wings stained glass. When Peter had last seen her, she had been young and green, but had since changed colors like leaves preparing for winter. He could feel her power as a heat shimmer in the air.

"Your Majesty," Peter said. He swept into a deep bow, remembering his manners from the fairy court. Opposite him, Hook awkwardly mimicked the gesture.

"You two again," the queen said. She had many large, crystalline red eyes and they fixed on Peter. "It's been a long time, Pan. I thought we were quite rid of you."

"I thought the same," Hook said, but stopped smiling when the queen's attention snapped toward him.

"And you, Hook," she said. "You hardly ever make trouble anymore. How is it that I find you preparing to disturb a fairy commune?"

"Madame," Hook protested, "I had no such intentions—"

"Quiet." The queen's wings snapped at the air, and the force of her magic washed over Peter, making his face throb.

Ernest, who had wrestled his way free of the stunned pirates, suddenly lunged to Peter's side and seized hold of his arm. Peter jumped, having forgotten about him. "Peter was helping me," he said nervously. "We came to get the magic flower to heal Curly. Hook attacked us. Peter was trying to save me."

"That's hardly fair," Hook said. "Pan and I have been having a friendly disagreement all day; I was merely bringing him my latest rebuttal—"

"Hook," the queen said. Her voice was like church bells, deep and ponderous. "Begone."

Hook looked like he might argue, but he deflated when the queen's red stare turned on him. He stepped back, beckoning to his crew. "Your neck has been saved this time, Pan," he called. "But you won't be so lucky next time."

Peter waved to him. Hook sneered back as he retreated, and was gone into the night.

"Come," the queen said briskly. "The commune

has already begun."

She led Peter and Ernest into the forest.

~~*

"Are you all right?" Ernest asked. "Did Hook hurt you?"

"Of course not," Peter said. He wished the fae hadn't interrupted them.

The fairy queen and her retinue were only a fraction of the fae attending the commune. As they walked through the woods, streams of fairies flew overhead and pearly light danced on the trees. The fae were converging on a single point in the distance.

Ernest had not let go of Peter's hand. The fairies seemed to make him anxious. "Do you think they'll let us leave?" he asked. "Now that we've seen where the commune is?"

"Yes," Peter said distractedly. "Shh." He was trying to eavesdrop on Tink and the fairy queen, who were flying along ahead. They were talking about him.

"I concede that he is your responsibility," the queen said. "But I do *not* understand why you had to bring him back here. He made his choice long ago."

"It was the wrong choice," Tink said. "I told you it was."

"He lived with it for ten years. Why not a lifetime?"

"Ten years isn't so long for a human," Tink said. "He wished for me, so I went."

The queen made a dismissive sound.

Peter frowned. Before he could think much more about it, they emerged into a grotto so bright it was like standing on the moon. The ground was carpeted in flowers of all kinds, from bluebells to vigorous lilies;

they rioted together, crowding and crawling over each other like weeds. In the center was a wide, squat tree with green leaves and white bark, its branches teeming with fairies.

Ernest stopped apprehensively at the treeline. Peter stopped too. "What's wrong?"

"Nothing," Ernest said. "Do you think they bite?"

"Of course they do," Peter said. "But they won't bite *you*. You're with me."

Tink flew back to join them. "And me," she said. "More importantly."

Peter grimaced at her and pulled Ernest into the meadow. It was impossible not to tread on the flowers; there were a million of them underfoot.

Already the commune tree was turning black as the fairies burrowed inside it, filling it with a hundred glowing, twisting channels. Peter had seen a fairy commune before, long ago, when he and the Lost Boys had first explored Neverland. The fae would eat their sacrificial tree from the inside out, each taking enough life from it to sustain them for a year of growing things. By night's end, the tree would be hollow and dry as bone.

A fairy landed on Peter's chest as they walked closer. It had a shiny black body and wings that turned green and gold as they caught the light. Its antennae shivered in the air. "Pan," it said, startled. "Welcome back."

The other fairies began to take notice of the human presence in their midst and came to investigate in an ominous, glittering swarm. Ernest gave a muffled whimper and tried to back away, but Peter kept a firm grip on him; the fae wouldn't trust someone who fled. They were wrapped in a mirage of wings, chimes, and trembling light, the touch of many small hands on their skin as the fairies settled upon them.

The fae of Neverland were quite a bit less human than the fairies in Peter's childhood storybooks: some had many legs and some none at all, some had eyes on stalks and some had clusters of iridescent eyes which all blinked at once, while still others had spines or fur or stingers or too many teeth. All of them had wings, but some were silken and some were filmy and white, as if they had been cut from butcher's paper. They chittered in the bell-like fairy language with accents of brass, silver, and crystal.

"So you've come for a flower," the queen said, landing on the back of Peter's hand. Even amid the other fae, her words carried, and her glow was unmistakable. "Which flower might that be?"

Peter and Ernest glanced around helplessly at the many varieties of flowers around their feet. "I don't know," Ernest said. "There wasn't any description."

"They want the flower that only grows on the night of the commune," Tink said smoothly. "The one with the power to cure any illness."

"Ah." The queen gave a sparkle of laughter as if she and Tinker Bell were sharing a joke. "Of course. Go and stand beneath the tree, Ernest. A bud will open when the moon is overhead. Pick it, and be careful not to spill the pollen. Not you, Pan," she added, as he started toward the tree. "Stay. I would have a word. Bell, see that Ernest finds his flower."

Tink flitted over to Ernest's shoulder. Ernest threw an uncertain look at Peter as he went, leaving Peter alone with the fairies.

"Why have you come back, boy?" the queen asked.

Peter blinked. He had the feeling she had asked him a riddle he didn't understand. "What's Neverland without me?"

"Many things to many people. What are you doing here?"

"I—had to come back and deal with the pirates."

The queen tilted her jeweled head. "They have as much right to be here as you, and have sailed these seas for many years. Why have you suddenly come to eradicate them?"

"They're villains," Peter said, vaguely annoyed. He could tell the queen wanted something else from him, but he didn't know what. "I'd have come back sooner if I'd realized everyone would let Hook take over."

"One might argue that they didn't mind being ruled by a pirate."

"Of course they minded," Peter snapped. "They just couldn't do anything about it, because *I'm* the only one who can stop him—"

"Enough," the queen interrupted. "I would speak plainly with you, Pan, but as you're beyond reason..." Her wings fanned louder, and the shiver of her magic washed over him—this time cold, a piercing cold that dug its nails into his head. "It's time you came back to yourself."

Her voice struck a note that made his teeth ache. "*Remember.*"

~~*

The night was clear and dazzling, and Peter had never been so afraid to breathe. He stopped every few minutes to listen, silent, to be sure that the house remained asleep.

He kept the drapes open, working by moonlight on the window seat to avoid lighting a lamp. Despite shaking hands, he was as quick with his needle as he had always been, shortening the hem of his stolen trousers so the cuffs wouldn't roll over his feet. As a child, Peter had thought nothing of running away in his nightgown; it was only a little lacier than the ones his brothers wore. Now, practically speaking, he needed a suit of armor to cover the way his body had changed. He had taken an old shirt and a pair of large trousers from his father's wardrobe, both baggy enough to conceal any shape.

In the moonlight, he slipped into his boy clothes. With his ensemble donned, he looked like a young man with an improbable quantity of thick brown hair. That was the last step: stretching open his sewing scissors and sawing off his hair. It took longer than he expected, several feet of unruly silk pouring to the floor around his shoes. When he was finished, his hair was hacked to just above his ears, and following its natural inclination to curl.

Peter stared at himself in the mirror, registering the terror in his eyes almost before he realized he was afraid. This was exactly what he wanted, and it was unforgivable.

If he stayed, he'd be in an asylum by the next evening. There was only one way out.

The latch gave easily, like it had been waiting, and Peter's window came open in a gust of cold air. Outside, the world looked ghostly. It was a fairytale night—thin clouds swirled like seafoam across a black ocean, stars like a fistful of glitter, all so close he could almost touch them. London seemed small, hunched down to the earth, while the sky hung low over the city and stretched out forever.

Peter stepped up on the window seat. It felt unsteady beneath his feet, until he realized it was him shaking. Doubt caught him off balance and he crouched, wrapping his arms around his knees.

At the back of his mind, he wondered if he really wanted to die, if he'd convinced himself he could fly to make it easier. Would his mother wake to find his body on the lawn, hair cut off, wearing his father's clothes? Would they take pictures of him for the papers?

Was that any worse than being found in his bedroom with all the evidence strewn around him, too much of a coward to make the final leap?

Peter pressed the heels of his palms into his eyes, pushing in until he saw spots. As he did, he heard bells.

They came from outside, faint and eclectic like a wind chime. Peter stuck his head out the window. There was a ball of silver light drifting down from above the trees in the yard. It was too large to be a firefly—the light was the size of his fist, and as it approached, he could see that the glow emanated from a body within.

With a gasp of disbelief, Peter stretched out to catch the fairy in his palm. It clung to his fingers with furred, segmented limbs, its white silk wings fluttering in the breeze. Holding his breath, Peter leaned back inside. The fairy crouched in his hand, antennae shivering.

"Hello?" Peter asked. He had to be dreaming, or worse, completely mad—dressed as a boy and talking to an insect. Maybe it was an unfamiliar species of moth, blown here by a strange wind.

Then the fairy opened her eyes. She had dozens of them, each glowing like a gas bulb. Her wings fanned suddenly, faster than he could follow, producing a shimmering sound like bells and chimes.

Without knowing how, Peter knew the sound was his name.

"You know me?" he asked.

"Of course I do," she said. Her wings shed a silty gray dust that gathered in his palm. "Don't you remember me?"

He shook his head, but as he did, a memory tugged at him. He knew her voice. This was the same fairy who had appeared, long ago, to take him to Neverland. He dredged up a name: "Tink? Tinker Bell?"

"That's more like it," she said.

She had changed. He remembered her fur being bright gold, but it had dulled to the steel gray of his grandmother's hair. Several of her eyes had gone dark or filmy white, but those that remained were glowing with impatience. "Are you ready to go?" she asked.

"Hold on." Peter took a deep breath, turning away and staring into his dim bedroom. He blinked hard and turned back to find Tink looking quizzical. "Am I dreaming?"

"You said the same thing last time," she said.

"You're going to take me back to Neverland?"

"As soon as you stop dithering, yes."

He lifted her to eye level, breath trembling in his lungs. "Can you promise me it's real?"

She gazed at him for a moment, something in her demeanor softening. "Yes," she said. "It's all real. You're not dreaming. Here, I'll show you."

She pinched his hand with two of her hind legs, hard enough that he yelped and clapped a hand over his mouth. From down the hall, he heard a creak of bedsprings, and his mother called: "Wendy?"

Panic shot through Peter and he stared at Tink, afraid she hadn't known. She just made a *tsking* noise and flew up to his shoulder. "Better go now," she said.

He heard his parents' door open and his father said, sleepy and suspicious, "Wendy? What was that?"

"Out the window!" Tink ordered, and Peter scrambled up on the windowsill. The sky seemed closer than ever, but the height of his window was as frightening as before. He made the mistake of looking down, and his stomach turned.

He shrank back inside. He heard his father try the door and find it locked. "*Wendy*!" A heavy fist slammed against the door, and Peter flinched, looking at Tink beseechingly. "I don't remember how to fly."

"Happy thoughts," she said curtly. "Fairy dust."

She flew above him in a rush of silk wings, showering him in silver sand. It slid over his cheeks and spread across his shoulders.

Peter stared at her. It seemed so absurdly childish, and so impossible. "Happy thoughts?" Neverland was a world away, buried in his memories, and there was nothing else.

"Think about going home," Tink said.

Peter shut his eyes. His father's fists hammered on the door like distant thunder. He didn't think of home; he couldn't picture it.

He thought, *One way or another, it'll be over*.

Then he twisted toward the window and leapt.

~~*

"Oh, dear," the queen said.

Peter didn't remember falling to his knees, but he found himself looking up at her, his eyes blurry and his chest aching. The world around them had dimmed, everything gray and faraway except for the queen. "What did you do to me?"

"I wanted to see behind that shield of yours," she said. "Now I understand why you keep it up."

Peter swallowed hard, trying not to cry. An awful, drenching awareness had overtaken him. He found he was shaking, both with anger and with a bone-deep fear he had forgotten about until that moment. It hit him, again, that his skin didn't belong to him, that he was a puppeteer moving a stranger's body. That he was playing a character, while the real, lonely, frightened Peter was buried inside him.

"I didn't want to remember," he choked out. "Why did you make me?"

The queen studied him like a scientist with a specimen. "This world is mine to protect, Pan. Dreamers are always welcome here, whatever their reasons. But you seem insistent on tearing the world apart in all your fantasies."

"That's right," Peter spat. "I'm here to fight. I'm a *boy*."

"So you are," she said. "When do you intend to grow up?"

Grow up. Peter heard the words echoing in his father's voice, and it was too much. Fury overwhelmed his fear, burning the awareness away in a red haze. He lunged at the queen, only to have the world come back into focus around him in a surge of color. He realized he was surrounded by the queen's retinue, and all of them were bristling with stingers, barbs, and poison teeth.

"Be careful, Pan." The queen had not moved. "Much of this world will bend to your desires, but I will not. How would you like to be banished from Neverland forever?"

"*No*," Peter snarled.

"Then calm yourself," she said. "I will leave you to your dreaming, so long as Neverland survives it. Think on that."

She rose, and the other fairies went with her, returning to the commune tree. The moon was climbing behind them, a glaring white disc in the night sky.

Ernest gave an excited shout from the tree and came hurrying back to Peter, cradling a star-shaped white flower. A well of silver dust trickled through the petals, streaming his Ernest's fingers. "This is it!" he said breathlessly. "Look—isn't it beautiful?"

Peter looked, but found he couldn't share Ernest's enthusiasm. The quest felt suddenly stale, a story told so many times that the outcome was obvious.

The flower was a joke; the healing magic was just fairy dust. Tink had known it all along.

"Of course," Peter said wearily. "Let's go home."

Three

"I want to visit the mermaids," Curly said, and the Lost Boys let out a cheer. It had only been a day since Curly had drunk the flower tea, and he was already feeling well enough to get up and walk about, color back in his cheeks.

"You ought to take it easy," Ernest cautioned him. "You nearly died."

"Yeah, Curly," Tootles said. "Let us kiss the mermaids for you."

A friendly but violent tussle followed this exchange, with Ernest wading in to stop the fighting and remind everyone that Curly was still too newly recovered to be beaten up. Peter sat on a branch above, watching the exchange and playing listlessly on a set of reed pipes he'd discovered in the hideout.

The Lost Boys had fully warmed to him after he and Ernest had returned with the magic flower, treating Peter with the same reverence they had when he was a boy. That was the trouble. It was the *same* reverence. Nothing about them had really changed in the decade he had been away.

Ernest was the only one with any backbone or authority, and even he had started treating Peter with friendly regard, deferring to him more often than not to keep the peace. He had said nothing more about their encounter with the fairies, except to describe the fairy queen and her retinue in awed tones. The Lost

Boys wanted desperately to see the next fairy commune. Peter never wanted to see one again.

In fact, there was nothing he really wanted to do. Peter knew all the games the Lost Boys played, all the places they visited, all the beasts they battled. They still had fun, but it was the same fun. They had no real fears, no want for anything new. Peter had no explanation for why, unlike the rest of them, he had been struggling to sleep—no explanation for the anxious buzzing in his head.

Only Tink seemed conscious of his foul mood. She had been quiet, studying him like a phenomenon she didn't understand.

She flew up to join him on the branch when she grew tired of watching the Lost Boys brawl. "You're sulking," she said.

Peter shrugged her off his shoulder. "Am not."

"If you're so bored with the Lost Boys," she said, "why don't you kill them?"

Peter stared at her.

"Or do something else. But stop moping."

"I'm *not* moping," he said. He watched her crawl over his knee, then stared off at the mountains.

"What do you want?" Tink asked. "What would help?"

"If I could forget everything." His memories had retreated to a distant haze, but they had left him with a nagging awareness he couldn't shake off and didn't understand. Every time he caught a glimpse of his reflection, something in him flinched.

Tink said nothing, but sat there cleaning her fur. Peter had the feeling she was at a loss, and he hated it. It reminded him of something else he didn't want to remember—the feeling of people who cared about him unable to understand what was wrong with him, unable to fix it.

~~*

"I want to be Peter Pan today," John said.

"And I wanna be Captain Hook," Michael said in his gummy, four-year-old speech, holding up one of his little hands with a single finger bent in the shape of a claw.

Peter glared at John. Peter was already wearing the green tunic and trousers that constituted Peter Pan's costume in their nursery games; he had even tried pulling up his hair today, twisting it into a knot at the back of his head so it looked shorter. "Michael, you're not big enough to be a dread pirate," he said. "And *I'm* Peter Pan."

"You're always Peter Pan," John drawled. "It's my turn. Actually..." *Actually* was John's favorite word. As he said it, he pushed his glasses up his nose with the air of someone being painstakingly rational. "If you're being fair, it should be my turn for the next month, because you've been Peter Pan at least thirty times."

"If you're being fair," Peter said, "I invented Peter Pan, so I get to decide who plays him. And besides, the tunic doesn't fit you."

"Who cares? I can wear something else." John stole Peter's wooden sword from the toybox and brandished it. "Come on, Wendy. I'm sick of being Hook and having you slice me to ribbons." He grinned, but Peter didn't smile back. "Why don't you play my fairy?"

"Give me that sword," Peter said coldly. "You're not playing Peter Pan, and that's final."

51

"Yes I am," John said, hopping back a pace. "Try and stop me."

Peter tackled him to the floor, knocking John's glasses off and nearly crushing them with his elbow as he tried to grab the sword away. John yelped, pulling on a fistful of Peter's hair and flailing his sword arm out of reach. Michael, who was used to his siblings brawling, watched with interest.

Nana the dog, however, woke from a doze to see her children fighting and began to bark in distress. Within moments, Peter heard their mother's footsteps on the stairs to the nursery. "Children?" she called. "Is everything all right?"

John looked triumphantly up at Peter. "I'm going to tell her that you're being unfair," he said. "And then you'll *have* to play someone else."

He was right. Mrs. Darling was very concerned about fairness, especially when it came to how Peter treated his brothers. "You must learn to be more gracious, dear," she said worriedly, inspecting John's glasses to make sure they hadn't been bent. "Let your brother play—who is it? Peter Pan? That's such a wonderful name. I think it suits John very well, don't you?"

"It's my name," Peter ground out. "I don't care if it suits John. It's *my* name."

"Dearest," Mrs. Darling said, "you're taking this very seriously, don't you think?"

~~*

Peter jerked upright in the dark, heavy furs sliding down to pool around his waist. The room smelled of dirt and wood smoke, nothing like the soap and pastel paint of the nursery in his dream. Still, Peter reached out for confirmation, and his questing hand found a warm shoulder.

"Hello?" Ernest mumbled. "Peter?"

Peter let out a breath he didn't know he been holding upon hearing his name.

"It's me," he said shakily. He knew where he was. This was the old hideout. In a concession to their new friendship and co-leadership of the Lost Boys, he and Ernest were sharing the largest bed.

"What's wrong?" Ernest asked, his voice thick with sleep.

"I'm bored," Peter said. That wasn't quite true, but he had no other name for his trembling unease; it was a distant panic he was putting off feeling. "Let's go find that kraken that lives under Death's Head Cavern. I want to know if it can really eat a man whole."

"No," Ernest said. "Let's not."

"Why not?"

"I don't want to get eaten."

His calm logic raised Peter's hackles more than usual. "Fine," he said. "Stay here, then. *I'm* going to do something interesting."

He scrambled out of bed, ignoring Ernest's muffled protest.

~~*

At first, Peter didn't know where the impulse was taking him. He flew out in the first light of dawn and caught a breeze blowing toward the water. It carried him far across the clouds until the sea stretched below. It was only when he saw the black sails of the *Jolly Roger* that he knew why he had come. He had almost forgotten about the war he was going to fight.

The *Jolly Roger*'s sails were full, her course set for somewhere on the other side of Neverland. There was a familiar figure standing at the helm, and Peter's heart cracked open at the sight of him, letting in a trickle of excitement. He pitched himself through the wind and came down silently on the banister behind Hook.

Hook was humming to himself, his hand upon the ship's wheel. He was dressed in a maroon coat this time, embroidered with dark, labyrinthine stitching that occasionally resembled ships' rigging, cresting waves, or creatures of the deep. His hat was trimmed with peacock feathers. Peter cocked his head, wondering who Hook had to impress with that outfit.

Everything about Hook seemed a little frivolous, yet perhaps that was the point of it. He was such a dastardly villain that he could stand to do everything in twice as many ruffles as the next man.

He also had a pleasant singing voice, deep and on-key, and the tune he was carrying was a cheerful one. Peter sat listening for a while, until the urge to be noticed became overwhelming.

"You should watch your back, Captain," he said.

Hook jumped. He turned, slowly, attempting to look like he hadn't been startled. "You again," he said.

"Me," Peter said. He slid from the banister. The deck rolled gently beneath his bare feet, the wood polished smooth and glossy. The pirates seemed to have flourished without him; the ship was impeccable.

So was Hook. If being stabbed in the ribs still affected him, he gave no sign of it. He stood there with haughty poise, looking down his hawkish nose at Peter. "I should thank you," he said. "It's been a long time since anyone managed to take me by surprise. It's been a long time since anyone did *anything* interesting around here."

After what he had seen of the Lost Boys, Peter wasn't surprised, but it warmed him a little to hear Hook say it. "I'll show you something interesting," he said.

He took a step forward, and Hook drew his sword, holding it extended between them.

"If you're here for a fight, I can certainly provide one," Hook said. "But I thought you might have reconsidered dueling me after last time."

"Shut up," Peter said. "It wasn't a fair fight." He was, now that he'd thought of it, itching for a rematch. Just the thought of battle made him feel like his body was coming back into alignment, pushing away the worst of his memories and leaving him keen. He could prove himself against Hook.

Ernest had given him a sword, a long, thin blade like the ones the pirates fought with. Peter drew it from its sheath ponderously, keeping his eyes fixed on Hook, or more accurately on the way Hook watched him. It was strangely exhilarating to see himself observed as an enemy, as a threat.

"I had rather hoped you might be willing to talk," Hook said.

"I don't like talking. I like fighting."

Hook's lip curled in a smirk. "You always were a vicious brat."

Peter grinned and lunged, swinging his sword in a broad arc that should have cut across Hook's chest. Instead, Hook ducked effortlessly away, quicker on his feet than Peter had imagined he could be. The next time Peter swung at him, Hook caught his sword at the junction of his own hilt and blade, locking it there and then throwing his wrist out to the side, turning the blow and Peter with it. The flat of his sword slapped Peter across the back, sending him stumbling.

"Surely you can do better than that," Hook said.

Peter's ears burned with humiliation. "I'm going to cut you up," he said, "and feed you to the sharks."

"Well, do it then. Or are you all talk?"

Peter surged toward him again. Their swords met with a force that made him grit his teeth, reverberations running up his arms, his muscles tensing and locking when his strength matched against Hook's and began to give way. He simply couldn't force his way through Hook's guard—and it had never been his style to try, but something about Hook's taunting had made Peter want to meet him head-on, cut through him. Instead, he found himself being pushed back toward the railing, and in a flash remembered how Hook had managed to pin him to the tree before.

He couldn't let that happen again. It was *his* turn to win, his turn to make Hook sweat and struggle and give in.

He yelled and threw himself forward, slipping through Hook's defenses and nearly managing to stab him in the gut. Hook parried, but he was retreating, Peter chasing him. Then they were dueling in earnest. Peter lost track of everything but the sound of their blades ringing together, clashing so viciously that the impact of Hook's every blow traveled through his body like a shock. There was nothing but the moment, and the next moment, the deadly flash of Hook's blade. Peter's movements were almost beyond his control— as if he were narrating the actions, but his body was completing them on its own, tuned to Hook's advances and reacting before Peter could think to.

Slowly he gained ground, forcing Hook to retreat down the stairs to the main deck. Hook stumbled on the last step, and Peter saw his opening. He locked their swords together, twisted, and sent Hook's blade skittering away across the deck. In the next moment, he caught Hook in the stomach with his elbow and knocked him back against the railing, flicking the point of his sword up beneath his chin.

Hook froze, breathing hard, and for a moment they stared at each other.

Peter was drenched in sweat, his arms tingling with exhaustion. "I win," he panted, grinning. He slowly lowered his sword to aim at Hook's heart. One thrust, and it would be over. Peter wet his lips with his tongue. "This is it. You're mine."

"Am I?" Hook asked, as Peter drew back his sword. "Or are you mine?"

The blow came from behind. A shattering *thump* across the back of Peter's skull made the world burst white, then black.

~~*

Someone was playing the piano, a soft, melancholy tune. Peter's head throbbed, a singular point of pain resonating through his skull, and it took effort to pry open his eyes.

When he did, he stared into the dark of a blindfold. Peter twisted at the bindings on his wrists, grunting when he found them too tight to budge. He had been trussed like a pig.

"Ah," Hook chuckled, "he wakes."

The piano stopped, and footsteps approached. A

cold iron hook slid between the blindfold and Peter's forehead, pulling the cloth up. The first thing Peter saw was Hook, leaning over him with a lit cigar between his fingers. He smiled at Peter, beatific, his eyes like blue glass.

Then he stepped back, and Peter took in what had to be Hook's cabin. It was all red and gold, velvet and silk. Rich tapestries covered the walls; a grand piano stood beneath stained-glass windows overlooking the sea. Racks of jeweled swords, knives, and hooks covered an entire wall. Treasure was heaped in overflowing chests all around the room, glazed in the light of a chandelier that swung lazily above Hook's desk.

It was another world, one which did not belong to Peter at all.

Even the chair he had been placed in was beautiful. It was made of lustrous burgundy wood, and the arms were carved into the tails of mermaids. No, mer*men*. Their bodies arched into the curves of the chair, arms stretched helplessly above their heads, staring up at Peter with handsome faces and vacant eyes.

"Comfortable?" Hook asked.

"What are you doing with me?" Peter rasped.

"I seem to have lured you into a trap," Hook said. "I rather suspected you'd be too single-minded to notice Samuel waiting for you to turn your back."

"You're a coward."

"All's fair in war." Hook tickled the underside of Peter's chin with his claw. Peter's breath caught in his throat. "Don't worry, Pan. I've no intention of simply killing you—or at least no intention of killing you simply." He smiled. "I don't suppose you remember our history with crocodiles?"

"I cut off your hand and fed it to one."

Hook chuckled. "Indeed. Some years ago I stumbled upon the place where the beasts congregate. It's a part of the coast known as the breeding place for all kinds of monsters, and I thought it would be a wonderful place to have my worst enemies devoured. At the time, I didn't have anyone worth killing with such flourish. But now... I have you." There was something almost fond in his face. "You'll appreciate it, won't you?"

"Do your worst," Peter said. He had never meant anything more. The feeling of the ropes binding him tight was almost better than the feeling of dueling Hook. It was a fight he didn't know how to win, a danger he couldn't escape. That was good. He felt like a string that had been pulled taut after lying slack a long time.

"I'll kill you when you run out of tricks," he said.

Hook looked amused. "You've changed, Pan," he said. "Yet you're still quite the dramatist."

"Look who's talking."

"I admit it," Hook said. "But you love a good fight, don't you?"

Peter's stomach fluttered. "Yes."

"We have that in common, you and I," Hook said. "You know, I'm glad you've come back—" Someone thumped on the cabin door, and his head jerked up. "*What*?"

A pirate with sleek brown hair and thick arms pushed open the door. "We're approaching the Bitter Coast, Captain," he said.

"Perfect." Hook sprung out of his chair. "Thank you, Samuel." He tugged the blindfold back down over Peter's eyes. Grasping Peter by the ropes that lashed his arms to his sides, he lifted him from the chair and dragged him out on deck.

Wherever they had sailed, the air was colder here. Peter could hear waves crashing on the *Jolly Roger*'s hull, and the cheerful conversation of at least a dozen pirates who must have gathered to observe Peter's fate.

His ankles were bound together so he hung from Hook's grip. "I'd have you walk the plank," Hook said, his mouth close to Peter's ear, "but you'd struggle to do even that."

"I'll be back."

Hook laughed. "God, I hope so."

He tossed Peter onto the deck. "Throw him overboard," he said, and several strong hands lifted him to a dizzying height before pitching him over the side.

The wind howled past Peter as he plunged, unable to fly with his arms and legs bound. He yelped with pain and cold as he struck the water and went under. Saltwater rushed into his mouth.

The current pulled his blindfold askew, uncovering one eye. He bobbed back to the surface, twisting and straining to keep his head above the water. Through blurry vision, he saw the studded backs of crocodiles sliding toward him through the water.

His hands were already numb in the icy water. There was no way he could get them free. Above, the pirates were cheering and clapping, and as panic washed over him, Peter began to thrash. He barely had time to scream as something closed around his foot and dragged him under the water.

His blindfold came off completely as the sea closed over his head, and he opened his eyes to see a pair of scaly hands wrapped around his ankle. A mermaid's iridescent eyes stared up at him from the water below. She smiled and pulled him deeper.

A crocodile lunged at Peter through the water, jaws open, and another mermaid whipped between them in a flash of green scales, striking the beast a staggering blow with her tail. A rush of other merfolk swam past him, straight for the remaining crocodiles. The water erupted in a flurry of bubbles and blood.

Four

The beach stank of seaweed and brine, and so did he. Peter gagged up a lungful of saltwater, then fell on his face in the sand and lay in the beating sun while the merfolk chittered and compared wounds. One of them nudged at his toes with a rubbery cheek.

Slowly, Peter pushed himself up and wiped sand from his cheeks. He turned to wave at the merfolk, who were lounging in the shallows, flipping their tails from side to side and grinning at him. They didn't speak any language he understood, but they waved back, tossing their glistening manes.

"There you are," Tink said.

She came floating down from a tree branch on her gossamer wings. She landed on Peter's shoulder, and then picked up her feet with some distaste, inspecting the wet sand that had come off on them.

"Did you send the mermaids?" Peter asked.

"You're welcome," she said. "You're lucky I know Hook."

Peter grinned at her. "Thanks." Now that he had survived the crocodiles, he didn't know why he'd ever doubted he would.

Tink flicked sand at him. "There's seaweed in your hair."

Peter pulled himself up with a wince. "Let's get back to the Lost Boys," he said. "Hook did his worst. Now it's my turn."

~~*

The Lost Boys remembered how to play war, even if they didn't have quite the same boyish enthusiasm for it that they had ten years ago. Peter marshaled them as soon as he returned to the hideout, directing them to sharpen their weapons and begin scouting the forest. They made excellent spies, having the practice and personal hygiene to blend in with the natural environment.

Hook wasted no time. Early the next morning, when Peter was finishing breakfast, Nibs came rushing back to the hideout. "Pirates!" he cried. "Three of them."

Peter jumped to his feet. "What are they doing?"

"They were digging up treasure," Nibs said excitedly. He was getting into the spirit of war. "They were awfully close to our territory."

"Peter," Ernest said. He was frowning. "Even Hook can be reasoned with. I'm sure if you sent him an olive branch, he'd accept it."

"Why would I want to send him an olive branch?" Peter asked, annoyed. Ernest was good fun, in his way, but Peter wasn't about to let him stop the most exciting thing that had happened since his arrival in Neverland. "He's a *pirate*. If he's going to invade our territory, he'll pay the price. Come on!"

~~*

Though it had been a long time and Peter was taller now, stronger and bigger, he still remembered how to soften his footsteps when stalking prey.

He could hear the pirates singing. There were three voices, all gruff and all merry, and their owners were stamping through the forest with no regard for the noise they were making. As a young boy, Peter hadn't known what rum smelled like; now he did, and he knew the pirates reeked of it. As he crept closer, he could almost taste the salt in their beards and the tang of old blood on their swords. Flattening himself against the mossy trunk of a tree, he peered around and saw them: two pirates hauling a large chest that dripped chains of gold, a third acting as a sort of guide who was trying to juggle a sword, a map, a shovel, and the treasures which kept overflowing from the chest and tumbling to the forest floor.

Peter flitted after the pirates as they hummed and trundled through the trees. He had flown overhead and sighted the boat they were headed toward, tethered at the beach where the air sang of gulls.

They were not to reach it.

The guide fell behind a step as he fumbled with his map, trying to turn it over and trace a path to the sea. The other pirates meandered on. "I can feel the sea wind," one of them called. "There's no doubt it's this way."

"And I say we make sure," the guide said, rather petulantly. He was an anxious-looking man. When the others continued on without him, he cursed to himself and dropped the shovel, tucking the sword beneath his arm as he unfurled the map.

Peter flew forward, stopping just behind the pirate. He made no sound, but the displacement of air ruffled the hair on the back of the guide's neck, and the man twisted around with a gasp.

A single sweep of Peter's knife cut his throat. The

blood that burst forth was extraordinary, a spray of red that shot up like a fountain. The pirate died with nothing more than a gurgle and a thump as he hit the ground.

His companions looked around and saw Peter there, red to the waist, and both began to scream. They probably would have liked to think they were bellowing war cries, Peter thought.

He leapt over the guide's corpse toward them, and the two pirates scrambled back. They threw down the treasure chest, which fell on its back, sloughing gold. When they turned to run, the Lost Boys emerged from the trees, blocking them in.

The end was swift.

~~*

"My God," Tootles said. "I think that was Billy." He rolled the guide's body over, and several Lost Boys looked stricken.

"He brought us messages from Hook," Ernest said. "He wasn't bad."

"He was a pirate," Peter said, exasperated.

"That's right," Nibs said. The other boys glanced at him sharply, but he shrugged. "It's been a long time since we had a good fight."

Peter had the Lost Boys haul all three corpses to the beach, where they found the dinghy the ill-fated pirates had been attempting to reach.

"Let's return Hook's pirates to him," Peter said, and they piled the bodies in the boat, pushing it off the beach and back out to sea. Several of the boys watched it drift away.

In the treasure chest, they found an enormous

quantity of golden plunder and cut jewels, along with an assortment of fine weapons. Peter took a long knife with a glittering hilt and let the boys divide everything else between them. They feasted around the fire that night, everyone in a reckless, noisy mood. Only Ernest refused to celebrate. He got up before the meal was done and trudged away between the trees.

Peter went after him. "What's wrong with you?" he asked.

"I don't want to do this," Ernest said, his shoulders tight. "I *hate* fighting."

"Why are you such a coward?"

It didn't have quite the impact Peter was hoping for; he had been halfway hoping to start a fight, wanting Ernest to get mad at him and stop being so thoughtful and concerned. But Ernest frowned and lowered his head, and Peter felt the wind go out of his own sails.

"I made the truce with Hook because I didn't want anyone to get hurt," Ernest said. "You've ruined it."

"You can't stop people from being hurt."

Ernest's face twisted. "That's no excuse for not trying. You don't even want to try. I don't know why I thought anything different. You *liked* it when Hook was trying to hurt you."

"What?"

Ernest bit the words out like he had been chewing on them for days. "I keep thinking about it. Up on the mountain, when he attacked you—it was like you were enjoying it."

"Of course I was," Peter said, put off by his accusing tone. "I love fighting. What's wrong with that? All the other boys do too."

"Not like that," Ernest said.

"You're sore because you're the only one who's not acting like a man."

"What's being a man got to do with it?" Ernest snapped. "Maybe there's just something wrong with you."

Peter had to laugh. He had never felt less wrong in his life. "You can leave if you want," he said. "I won't make you fight."

Ernest's fists clenched at his sides. "I won't abandon the Lost Boys," he said coldly. "I'm not like you."

~~*

Ernest took the floor that night instead of sharing the bed, ignoring Peter when he spoke.

Peter didn't know what to do. Ernest's disapproval was draining the Lost Boys' enthusiasm, and worse, it was ruining Peter's fun. There seemed to be no dragging Ernest along with the game, but Peter liked him too much to banish him.

When Ernest got up to dress the next morning, still in a foul temper, Peter threw a pillow at him. "I'll fight Hook alone if you want," he said.

Ernest glared at him. "I don't want you to fight alone," he said.

"You don't want to fight with me, either," Peter retorted. "And someone's got to take care of Hook. But I don't need help if you don't want to."

Ernest folded his arms and walked over to the bed where Peter sat, his mouth pressed into an anxious line. "I wish we could do something else instead."

"There's nothing else I want to do," Peter said. "I want to *fight*." He hit Ernest with the other pillow for emphasis.

Ernest let out a slow breath. Then he tackled Peter back onto the bed, taking advantage of Peter's surprise and wrestling him into a hold. "*We* can fight," he said in a tone somewhere between frustration and reluctant affection.

"That's more like it," Peter said, elbowing him in the gut. Ernest's grip loosened, which let Peter thrash his way free, and then they were off, grappling back and forth across the bed. Ernest was as strong as Peter and larger, but less ruthless, so neither of them had any particular advantage.

Before long they were both sweaty, battered, and sporting extremely messy hair, but the fight was nowhere near ending when the screaming started.

It was not a playful scream. It was a bloodcurdling, awful, anguished sound, and it came from outside the hideout.

Ernest tore free of Peter. "What's that?"

Peter was already on his feet and sprinting up the stairs. The Lost Boys were clustered around a tree across the clearing, and Peter shoved between them. When he saw what their bodies had concealed, he stopped dead.

Slightly had always worn an expression of vague superiority; now his face was somber, his eyes gone as dull as marble, his glasses hanging off his nose. A sword with a whorled hilt and gleaming blade was stuck through his chest and driven deep into the tree behind him, holding his body upright. There was a note pinned to the front of his shirt, one corner soaked in the blood that had spilled and dried all down his chest. Tink was perched on his cheek, silently inspecting him.

Peter walked forward wordlessly and tore the note from Slightly's shirt. It was written in a beautiful curling hand and deep red ink. It said:

To the Lost Boys:

And so our truce is ended. I would have been happy to spare you in deference to our long and profitable peace, but your allegiance to Peter Pan means that we are now at war. Since you were so kind as to send me evidence of your intentions, I have endeavored to do the same.

I look forward to our next meeting.

Yours sincerely,
Jas. Hook.

"*Hook*." Ernest's voice was thick with loathing and grief.

Peter stared at the note. He knew he shouldn't have felt betrayed, but for a moment he couldn't move, wondering how Hook could have done this to him.

"If only you hadn't killed those pirates, Peter," Nibs whispered. "Hook hasn't bothered us in such a long time. He's just been out at sea."

Peter whirled toward him, furious and hurt, so suddenly that Nibs flinched away. "*What* did you say?" The Lost Boys stared at him, and whatever they saw, they were muted by it.

"If only you hadn't killed those pirates," Ernest repeated.

Peter rounded on him, and the look of quiet

resentment on Ernest's face was a stab at his heart. "What's wrong with you?" Peter demanded. "It's not my fault. It's *Hook*. You never should've stopped fighting him."

"We could never win without you," Nibs said tremulously. "And Hook didn't care about us, anyway. He only wanted you. He left us alone."

"Look at Slightly!" Peter cried. "Is that what leaving you alone looks like?"

"Peter," Tink said. "Stop."

The other boys shrank from him, except for Ernest. "It wasn't bad before," Ernest said. "It wasn't bad until you came back. And now Slightly's dead." Peter saw stubborn tears hanging in his eyes. "Who cares about your stupid war?"

"Now, boys," Hook said. "Don't fight."

Peter spun toward his voice, and a knife struck him in the chest.

Five

Tink made a shrill sound of alarm, and Ernest flung himself in front of Peter, drawing his sword.

"I'm fine," Peter snarled. He felt no pain; the dagger was as slim as a dart and hadn't gone deep. He jerked it out by the hilt as the pirates emerged from the trees, surrounding them. Hook, smiling, still had a hand raised from having thrown the knife.

"Why, my dear fellow," he said. "You don't look as if you were prepared for war after all."

"Run," Ernest said, pulling Peter back toward the hideout. "Everyone, *run*!"

The Lost Boys scattered, but Peter tore furiously out of Ernest's arms. Hook had taken something of his, and ruined their game, and he was going to pay for it. Over Tink's protests, he leapt into the air and drew his sword, preparing to dive down at Hook.

But halfway through the leap, Peter fell like stone, crashing to the ground and rolling to a stop.

Tink scrambled over his chest, shimmering in alarm. There was a sharp, throbbing pain where the knife had stuck in him. Peter looked down to see the corners of the wound turning yellow. A strange, tingling sensation spread through his limbs, and they felt heavy and weak when he tried to push himself up.

"You may want to attend to that," Hook said from above him. "I hear it can be quickly fatal."

"Fly!" Tink snapped, spreading her wings wide and

showering him in fairy dust. It took extraordinary effort for Peter to leave the ground, all the same; he scrambled away from the pirates, who were jeering and laughing, and kicked off. He clawed his way into the air like he was swimming, and a gust of wind swept him up and carried him over the trees.

The power of flight did not last him long. The pain in his chest was growing sharper and hotter by the moment, until he couldn't see through it. He half flew, half fell back to the earth, tumbling between the trees and sprawling on his back. He was sweating, burning up, and his stomach writhed. He turned over and vomited.

"Peter!"

His heart was horribly loud in his throat, and beating too fast. Cramps spread from his stomach into his chest, shoulders, and arms. He sucked in a deep breath, but his lungs were squeezing closed. He gasped frantically, every breath seeming shallower than the last.

The urgency in Tink's voice cut through his panic. "*Peter*!"

He looked up at her through tears of pain, barely able to move. "What do I do?"

"I know that poison," Tink said. "The only antidote is the one he carries with him."

Peter caught a glimpse of the cut through the gash in his shirt. It was festering green, turning black, and the sight made him throw up again. He was boiling, his throat and cheeks going dry and flushed.

"Am I going to die?" he moaned.

Tink stared at him with her glowing eyes, deep sorrow in them. She shook her head and came to him in a whisper of wings.

"I can slow the poison's spread," she said, "but you must get the antidote within a day. Do you understand?"

"Yes," Peter croaked, "but what are you—"

She blazed suddenly like a candle, a bright point of light that hurt to look at. Silver thread spun around the wound and smoke poured from the tear in his skin, squeezed out as the flesh knitted together behind it. Tink flared so bright he had to look away, and then at once the light went out.

Peter turned his head back and saw, for a moment, silver dust suspended in the shape of her silhouette before she blew apart and was gone.

~~*

He sat still for a long time, watching the fairy dust slide through his fingers, as fine as silt.

He felt hollow. All around him, the world was still and dead, as if he were the last thing left alive. No matter how tightly he squeezed his palms together, the thin pool of dust gradually escaped him, blown away by the breeze or tracing its way between his fingers.

"I do believe in fairies," he whispered, and it sounded so small and lonely that he said nothing else.

All children lost their fairies when they grew up. Peter had always known that, but as with many things, he had seemed to be the exception. He had been charmed, lucky in everything, stronger and braver and quicker-witted than the other boys. The fairy on his shoulder had only emphasized his agelessness, his power over the world.

He felt helpless now, cradling what remained of

her in his hands, unable to get back one of the only things he had ever loved.

Whatever spell Tink had cast on the poisoned wound had stopped him being sick; the weakness and nausea had vanished instantly. He could still feel a curious heat around the cut, but it seemed to be trapped in place, not spreading through his blood. He wondered how long it would take for the stitches to come unbound, for the wound to fester again. It had happened so fast the first time.

He sat there frozen in dread of it, in fear of dying, and in worse fear that he would begin to cry and not be able to stop.

Six

The hideout had been burned to cinders. The clearing in which the great tree had stood was burnt to a shadow, the surrounding forest singed. There were no bodies; the Lost Boys were gone. Peter wasn't surprised. He'd have taken prisoners too, if he were Hook.

As he stood in the ashes, his misery hardened into determination. If nothing else, he had to rescue them; it was too late for Tink and Slightly, but he wouldn't let anyone else die.

All he had was his dagger, but that would have to be enough. He still felt strong, but the wound on his chest had grown a deeper, angrier red that purpled in the center. The silver stitches seemed to be straining to contain it.

The fae had heard from the sharks that churned the waters far offshore that Hook had plans for his captive Lost Boys. He was to lay a trail that led to Death's Head Cavern, where the rocks jutted up like teeth sharp enough to impale a man. A trap for Peter Pan, the fae reported. Hook intended to feed each and every Lost Boy to the great kraken that made its home in the depths of the cavern—and if Peter Pan wished to stop him, he was welcome to try.

Apparently Hook had loudly announced these plans to the wind and sea, confident that they would be overheard and reach Peter's ears somehow.

~~*

Death's Head Cavern lurked beneath a cliff that extended out over the sea, its sunken eyes staring from the tangle of algae and grime that coated the rocks. Its mouth was wide and grinning, large enough for a small boat to sail inside, although it quickly became too cramped and narrow for the boat to continue. From there on in, one had to proceed on foot, walking across the slippery stone floor and avoiding the razor-sharp teeth that continued far down the cavern's throat. Passages split off in every direction, continuing for miles in mazelike twists and turns, so that even the most expert navigator quickly became lost.

Peter had led the Lost Boys through these passages once, discovering a way they could go straight through to a pretty lake where bears and other beasts could be spied on. But there were other passages which had no exit, or which seemed to go on forever. In one of these was a pool that plunged deep below the earth, deeper than even Peter could swim, where a kraken lived. It could be called forth only by the taste of blood, but once summoned it was ravenous.

Peter hid close to the cave entrance and waited until he heard the pirates singing in their rowboats. One dinghy carried the Lost Boys, all bound and gagged such that they could hardly move, and a surly-looking pirate with an eyepatch. The other boats contained much of the *Jolly Roger*'s crew, including the one called Samuel and the captain himself. Hook was seated in the rear, wearing another ridiculous coat and an enormous hat covered in black ostrich feathers. He had the air of someone dressed for the opera, not a massacre.

His hand was occupied with a map that he spread across his knees, his iron hook pinning the map open as he traced some route through the caves. He seemed aloof to the grunting and straining of the men pulling the oars. But at a word from Samuel, he lifted his head and smiled from beneath the brim of his hat.

Peter watched as the pirates landed their boats where the channel became too thin to maneuver and the cave floor grew wide enough to walk upon. The Lost Boys had their feet bound together so that they could not even walk. Ernest looked as though he had been beaten; one of his eyes was swollen shut and there was blood in his hair. Peter's hackles rose at the sight. The Lost Boys were his. Hook had no right to touch them.

Peter stole from behind the stalagmite that had hidden him and followed the pirates. The twisting passage made it easy; all he had to do was stay one twist behind them.

When he was sure they had gone the right way and would soon be at the kraken's lair, he cut away down a side passage. The passage led up and up until it opened onto a narrow ledge above the kraken's pool, which was presently black and smooth, barely visible in the soft glow of the bone-white walls. Peter dropped to the cave floor and crouched behind a crest of stone across from the entrance.

A few minutes later, he saw yellow light dance across the walls as the crew emerged into the room with their captives. Hook alone seemed unaffected by the atmosphere of the cave; the other pirates were pale and nervous as they dragged the Lost Boys inside and shoved them to the floor.

"Well, my friends," Hook said with the air of an actor beginning a monologue. "I suppose now we find out whether your convictions are justified. I hope for your sake he's flying here right now, ready to snatch you from the jaws of the beast." He bent beside Ernest and took from his belt a small, gleaming knife, which he held out to Ernest's cheek. "Or else your blood will summon it from the gates of hell itself to devour you."

Even in the dark, Ernest's eyes shone with anger. Hook laughed and straightened up, turning away from the Lost Boys and addressing the pirates. "Be prepared. If Pan comes, he will be here any minute."

Peter crept silently along, making his way toward the boys with his knife in hand.

"Are you there, Pan?" Hook bellowed, loud enough for his words to glance off the walls and carry deep into the winding tunnels. "I'm going to blood them! The kraken will tear them apart!"

Nibs lay on his side by a large stalagmite, his hands twisted behind his back and bound together with heavy rope. He gave a tiny jump when Peter touched his shoulder, but lay still as Peter sawed through the ropes, not moving even when they gave way and he was freed. Peter circled around to free Tootles.

"This is your last chance, Pan!" Hook roared. "You have ten seconds to show yourself before the feast begins! Ten! Nine! Eight!"

The pirates were not watching the Lost Boys; they were facing the entrance or staring into the water, transfixed with fear and apprehension. Peter reached Ernest and cut through his bonds in one slice.

"Seven! Six! Five! Your boys are counting on you,

Pan!"

Ernest turned over and reached for the knife, jerking his head toward Curly, who lay on his other side. Peter gave him the knife.

"Four! Three! *Two*..."

Something heavy landed on Peter's back and knocked him to the floor beneath its weight. He struggled, but froze in shock when he realized it was Nibs holding him down. Curly and Tootles each grabbed one of his arms and twisted them until they felt like they would come out of their sockets.

Ernest put the knife beneath his chin.

Hook turned around and smiled.

"One," he said. "I'm afraid the kraken will have to go hungry."

~~*

They bound Peter hand and foot as they had the other boys. Peter could not speak as they tied him up. He felt hollow, like someone had scraped his heart and all the other meat from the inside of his ribs.

"Now, Pan," Hook said cajolingly. "You can hardly blame a bunch of clever young men for wanting to live."

Peter stared at the boys, who stood free of their bonds, awkwardly interspersed with the pirates and staring back at him as if they could not bear to look away. The only one who would not meet his eyes was Ernest.

Hook grabbed Peter by the shirt and dragged him to the pool's edge. He inspected the poisoned wound on Peter's chest and laughed at the sight of the silver threads. "What hard work the fairies wasted on saving you," he said. "Perhaps you'll poison the kraken as it eats you and I'll have killed two birds with one stone."

He cut a thin slice across Peter's palm—Peter heard Nibs gasp—and extended his blade out across the pool, letting Peter's blood sprinkle into the water where it spread like smoke.

Everyone held their breath for as long as they could, but there was no answer from the deep. Hook frowned slightly, then brought the blade to Peter's throat. "Very well," he purred. His breath was warm on Peter's ear. "It appears the beast wants a greater offering."

The knife brushed Peter's skin and parted it so easily that a thin line of blood ran down his neck without his even feeling pain. Then again, Peter wasn't sure he could feel pain anymore.

He was staring straight ahead, waiting for the deep cut that would end his life, when Ernest suddenly spoke: "Wait."

"Have you something to say to Pan before he dies?" Hook asked.

"To you," Ernest said. "You don't need to kill him. He'll join your crew with the rest of us."

Hook chuckled, and Peter felt the vibration on his ear. "Will he?"

"Yes," Ernest said. He took a step forward still clutching Peter's knife. "He will."

Hook was silent, as if considering. Then he gave a little sigh and said, "Ernest, my boy, you don't need him. You know that. You're all better off without him. He's the one who got you into this mess, brawling and killing when the rest of you were happy to live your lives in peace."

"That's true," Ernest said, and Peter's stomach

sank into his toes.

"Think how much happier you'd be with him gone," Hook said.

Ernest swallowed, and his eyes flickered. "The Lost Boys wouldn't be here without him," he said. "And if they weren't here... I'd be alone—"

"What does that matter now? They'd be dead without you. He abandoned them. Left them to fend for themselves while he ran away from Neverland." Hook's voice was gentle, reasonable. "Isn't that right, Peter?"

Peter nodded mutely, and felt the knife clip against his throat again. Blood rolled down his neck and Ernest gasped. "Be *careful*."

"You don't need him anymore," Hook said. "All you lack is his audacity. Let him go, and lead the Lost Boys yourself."

Ernest's shoulders were uneasy, his breath a little short. "I am leading them," he said. "And I want you to let him *go*. Now."

Hook groaned. "And here I thought we could avoid this kind of noble grandstanding. Very well." He glanced aside at Samuel and said, "Bind him. Feed them both to the Beast."

Two pirates stepped toward Ernest, but Ernest lunged at Hook, who must have then realized how close he was to the edge of the pool. He hastily dropped Peter on the ground and swung out of Ernest's path to avoid being knocked in.

The remaining Lost Boys snapped into action and charged after Ernest, slamming into the pirates and knocking them aside. They had no weapons, but they threw themselves upon the pirates anyway, wrestling with them for their knives and swords and guns.

Ernest landed on top of Peter, digging his knife beneath the ropes around his wrists and shearing through them with strong, sure motions. "I'm sorry, Peter," he said. "I'm sorry—"

Hook's sword plunged into his leg and Ernest fell away with a cry.

Peter broke from his daze at the sight of blood spilling from Ernest's thigh. He screamed and hurtled himself into Hook's feet, knocking him on his back and diving on top of him. Somehow Ernest's knife had found its way into Peter's hand and he drove it into Hook's shoulder, feeling him jerk and shout in pain. Peter ripped the blade free and swung it down for his throat, but someone seized him around the back and tore him off.

It was Samuel. As Peter rolled to his feet and Hook scrambled away, Samuel pulled his sword from its scabbard and attempted to spit Peter on the blade. Peter batted it aside and ran his knife through Samuel's chest in one sharp thrust.

Peter heard Hook's gasp as Samuel fell, lifeless, into the pool. His body struck the surface with a muted splash and sank instantly, dark water washing over the lip of the pool. His lantern, broken on the floor, left them in sickly firelight.

Hook was staring at the place where Samuel had stood with an expression of bewilderment. Peter could have stuck him with the point of his sword, he was sure, before Hook would've thought to react. But he was watching the procession of emotions that marched across Hook's face, from disappointment to sorrow to anger and back. All around them the boys and the pirates were shouting at each other, battling over stolen weapons, but their two captains were silent and still.

Then Hook grunted and stood straight, and Peter saw him quickly packing away each feeling like a host stuffing clutter into the closets before guests could arrive. When at last he turned to Peter, there was nothing in his face but contempt.

"So," Hook said. "You've broken one of my toys."

He drew his sword.

"Better to die than be a man called a toy," Peter said callously. The anger had gone out of him when it had plunged a blade through Samuel's chest; it had been replaced by something uglier, something that was almost grief, a grim inevitable feeling that the only way forward was to kill someone else. He knew that Ernest lay behind him, bleeding on the floor, and that he would do whatever it took to save him.

"I could say the same of that boy I killed," Hook sneered. "What was he to you? No more than a pawn."

"No. That was different."

"Was it?" Hook took a slinking step, like a tiger staring down its opponent. Peter could see his arm trembling under the weight of his sword, weakened by pain and injury. Peter's own wounds were barely hurting him; necessity and fairy dust had sharpened his body back into a tool he could use. Hook kept talking, probably trying to distract him. "Tell me, Pan, how was it different?"

"The Lost Boys aren't *mine*," Peter said. "And you killed Slightly while I was asleep. I killed your man in front of you."

"Good form," Hook said. There was a mean smile on his lips. "How about I return the favor and kill you in front of them?"

Peter lunged at him first, and Hook danced back,

evading the blade instead of deflecting it with his own. When Peter swung again, he directed his knife so that Hook had to parry it. He could see the shock of the impact travel up Hook's arm and into his shoulder, see Hook's teeth snap together to stifle a growl of pain. After several more blows, Hook's sword arm was trembling and weaving, though it did not fall. Peter leapt into the air and hurled his weight behind his knife, and meant to bring their blades together with such force as to make Hook drop his.

But Hook slid aside instead of taking the blow and Peter rushed past him, tumbling into the wall. Peter turned in time to see Hook—eyes burning, face twisted with effort—swinging for him again. Peter ducked, and Hook's claw rang off the wall, showering him with broken stone.

For several desperate moments he was fleeing, nearly suspended on the tip of Hook's blade as the captain forced him back, each piercing thrust of his sword almost reaching Peter's belly.

Then Peter tripped, and the wind caught him, and he billowed into the air like a sail catching the breeze and kicked the sword from Hook's hand. He was about to press his advantage, to drive his blade through Hook's chest, when Nibs screamed: "*Look out!*"

The pool's surface erupted. Two long, gray tentacles shot out from water in a spray, then came down on the floor with a sickening slap. The tentacles rippled with alien muscle as they hauled the rest of the kraken from the depths.

It had a bulging, scaly head and mottled gray skin, eyes that jutted up out of its face like those of an octopus. It smelled of carrion and seaweed, and as it rose over the pool, it stretched open a bloody mouth filled with icicle teeth. The maw was large enough to fit a man inside, end to end. By the looks of the scraps hanging from its teeth, it had just finished eating Samuel.

It screeched, an ear-splitting keening sound that made the cavern shake and Peter clap his hands over his ears. A wave of water washed over the cave floor as the kraken surged upwards, sending pirates and Lost Boys slipping and sprawling on the slick ground.

The kraken's hungry stare fixed on Ernest, who lay helpless in his own blood. The enormous jaws opened, the circle of jagged teeth spaced apart like gravestones and dripping red, and the kraken leaned down.

Peter flew across the room, dropping his knife and seizing Ernest's shirt in both hands, dragging him as he slid toward the entrance. The monstrous jaws snapped shut behind his feet, and Peter dropped Ernest beside Nibs and Tootles. "Get him out!" Peter screamed. "Run!"

Pirates shoved past them on their way out, not bothering with the Lost Boys. Peter turned to see the kraken snatch up a straggling pirate in one of its tentacles and drop him into its maw. Hook was running after Peter, his face twisted in a snarl. Peter grabbed a knife from Nibs's belt and leapt between the boys and Hook. Behind them both, the kraken dragged itself further from the water.

"It's coming for you, Captain," Peter yelled. "It's still hungry!"

Hook was pale with rage and terror. The Lost Boys disappeared down the passage and Peter stood in the entrance, unmoving as Hook sprinted the final distance. He didn't care if he got out as long as he stopped Hook from escaping.

Hook's sword was in his hand, and as he neared Peter, he swung. Peter parried, braced against the blade, shoved back. It was his strength against Hook's weakened arm; Hook fell away with a furious shout.

A shadow passed over his head. They both looked up to see the tentacle Peter had expected to seize Hook plunging down, instead, toward Peter.

He felt a hand grab the front of his shirt and yank him forward with such force as to send him sprawling—sprawling into Hook, who lost his balance and hit the floor beneath Peter. Where Peter had stood, the kraken's tentacle slammed into the rock, one of its coils shattering the entranceway and burying it in rubble.

Peter tried to rise, but Hook threw an arm over the back of his neck and dragged him back down.

"Together," he spat, "as always."

"Let go!"

"You think I'd let you escape and leave me?"

Peter threw himself into the air, dragging all of Hook's weight with him, narrowly in time to avoid being snagged by another enormous tentacle. He thrashed, but Hook wrapped an arm around his throat and clung to him as he hung in the air. The kraken turned its bulbous eyes toward them and reared higher out of the water, stretching open its awful mouth and screaming again. The cavern shook, dust and bits of rock falling from the ceiling.

Peter saw the ledge that led toward the remaining exit tunnel and flew toward it, straining under Hook's weight.

He clipped through the entrance just ahead of the kraken's suckered limb. He fell on the other side and was falling, head over heels down the slope as the tunnel collapsed behind them, Hook tumbling with him into the dark.

~~*

Peter lay stunned, blinking at the blackness that surrounded him, not knowing how long he had been unconscious. For a moment there was silence.

Then a bloodcurdling roar shook the ground beneath him, pebbles bouncing off Peter's head as they clattered farther down the tunnel. Peter heard a groan from nearby and forced himself up, fumbling at his belt for any weapon. He had nothing but his hands. Could he kill Hook with his hands?

He could try.

He scrambled toward Hook, only to be pitched over and sent sliding when another deep quake wracked the tunnel around them. He landed hard and rolled, unable to stop, battering his elbows and knees on the hard floor. He heard Hook falling over and over beside him before the tunnel finally spat them out. Peter hit the floor hard and it was a long moment before his spine stopped rattling.

"Hell's teeth," Hook moaned.

Peter dragged himself upright. He squinted into the darkness, trying to make out where Hook had fallen. All he could see was a sharp stalagmite jutting up to his left.

He grabbed the thin tip and snapped it off, leaving him with a spike several inches long and sharp as a needle.

He listened to Hook scuffling about. "Pan?" Hook asked warily. "Are you alive?"

Peter said nothing. He heard a muffled curse and then—with a soft huff of air—the ignition of a match. Flame burst from the end of a long, sturdy matchstick held in Hook's hand, throwing the cave into a sudden wash of light. Hook was still splayed on the ground.

He looked up, saw Peter standing there with the spike, and yelped.

The match went clattering away across the floor, firelight flaring, as Peter fell upon him. In answer to Hook's shout, the kraken gave another awful roar, this one more distant, and dust and bits of ceiling clattered down on Peter's head. But he barely noticed—he was busy trying to get the spike into Hook's throat while Hook grappled with him. Peter managed to clamber up Hook's chest and pin his shoulders with his knees, bearing down on him with all the weight of his body. He got the spike very near to Hook's throat but could not drive it in. Hook dug his nails into his wrist until his skin burned, and it took all Peter's will to keep gripping the spike. One hard push and Peter could kill him—but he couldn't do it.

The match was still lit, still clinging to life a few feet away, and with it Peter could see the piercing blue eyes staring up at him.

"Pan," Hook grunted. He did not look afraid. "Let me up, you fool. We can kill each other when we're out of here."

"I can kill you now," Peter snarled. He jerked forward and managed to scrape the point of the spike through the hair that grew along Hook's jaw. A line of blood pooled in his collarbone.

Hook drew a sharp breath. "You need my antidote."

"I'll take it when you're dead."

"I also carry more of that poison on my person. How will you tell the difference? Or will you drink one and pray your luck is good?" At Peter's hesitation, he tipped back his head, exposing his throat, and his grip on Peter's wrist slackened. "Go on, if you trust the coin toss."

Now there was nothing stopping Peter from driving the spike in, except that his body still wouldn't move. He could have done it in the heat of battle, but not when it was simply his choice. With Hook was staring at him, inviting him, Peter couldn't help imagining what would *happen* if he killed Hook. The blood, the silence, the shadows swallowing him up alone. He imagined how Hook's blue eyes would look if the life left them. He thought of Slightly's empty, dead stare and was suddenly nauseated.

He didn't want to kill someone again. Worse, he didn't want Hook to be dead. As the moments ticked by, he tried to convince himself that he did, but the idea broke over him in waves of increasing horror. He thought of Hook being gone the way Tink was, stripped out of the world, nowhere to be found.

That would be an empty world.

Hook looked as though he were getting a grim pleasure from this, watching Peter with such stark intensity that Peter wanted to look away. "I have a proposal," he said at Peter's continued silence. "You let me up, we find our way out of this cave, and then I give you the antidote."

"How do I know you won't try to kill me if I let you up?"

"Because only one of us can fly, and so it benefits me to keep you around."

Peter's instincts screamed for him to keep holding

Hook down. But there was something in his instincts that Peter did not trust. His instincts had led him to fight Hook in the first place. His instincts had led to war; they had gotten Tink and Slightly killed. His instincts twisted toward destruction, and he didn't even want his worst enemy gone.

He didn't want Hook gone.

Peter stood mechanically, dropping the spike to the cave floor. Hook got carefully to his feet. He looked down at Peter, his face in shadow.

Then, quicker than Peter could follow, he stepped forward and hit Peter so hard he fell over.

It was like getting struck by a plank; Peter crumpled on the floor, stunned. It was a moment before he had the sense to respond to having been attacked, reaching for the spike. By then Hook had turned away, clearly disinterested in pressing his advantage. He bent and picked up the fallen match.

"That was for Samuel," he said.

And Peter, whose fingers had just touched the spike, stopped.

He wrapped his arms around his knees instead, staring at Hook's back. Hook lifted the match to chest height, surveying the cave. He didn't turn around.

"Did you care for him?" Peter asked. He didn't know why he wanted to know, or even if he did, only that the words left his mouth before he could consider them.

Hook chuckled. It was an odd, bitter sound. "I suppose I did," he said. "We were lovers."

Peter's mouth fell open. He found he had nothing he could say.

"Which way is out?" Hook asked.

When Peter didn't answer, he turned around.

Peter pointed silently to the tunnel straight ahead of them, which had collapsed.

"Ah," Hook said. "Excellent."

Peter found his voice, though it came out faint. "There are other ways."

"Then lead us."

Peter got to his feet, wanting do something—anything—to apologize. But what could he say that would mean anything? *I'm sorry, I didn't think he mattered?*

And why should he feel sorry when Hook had killed Slightly first and been about to kill the others? He was angry with himself for feeling sick, for not being able to stop.

"This way," he said.

Seven

"Pan," Hook said. "Do you know where you're going?"

"Of course I do," Peter snapped.

But when he turned a corner and discovered the next twist in the route had collapsed, his mind went blank with panic. They had been walking for hours, discovering that passage after passage had caved in. The cavern Peter had once navigated so easily was almost unrecognizable.

Without thinking, he set a hand on the wall for support, and the darkness began to press in on him.

"Pan? What's the matter with you?"

"Nothing." Peter swung around and tried to take a step, but he slid to the floor instead, his pulse pounding in his ears. How long had it been since Tink's sacrifice? Twelve hours? Eighteen? He hadn't counted.

Hook *tsked*. "Where's that fairy of yours? She ought to give you another dose of pixie dust to keep you going."

Peter swallowed around a sudden lump in his throat. "She's dead," he said shortly. "She used the last of her magic to stop the poison from spreading. To give me time to find the antidote."

Hook sat across from him. It was a strange, abrupt movement, as if a weight had come down on his shoulders.

Peter watched, frowning, as Hook fumbled a cigar

from a pouch at his hip. He lit the cigar from his match and began to smoke, his brows drawn together.

"I didn't realize," Hook said at last. His voice had gone rough, like he was struggling to speak. "I'm sorry, Pan. I'm truly sorry."

"What do you care?"

"It may surprise you," Hook said, "but I considered her... a very good friend."

Peter blinked. "What?"

"Once we'd settled our differences over you, we got on quite well." Hook shot Peter a flat smile. "She always cared for you beyond reason. I should have known she'd protect you to the last."

If Peter hadn't known him better, he'd have thought Hook looked miserable. It was like looking in a mirror, and he didn't know what to make of seeing his own grief in the face of his enemy.

"How... how did you know her?"

"Through you, obviously." Hook picked at the label on his cigar. "She protected the Lost Boys after you left—keeping them alive in your honor, I suppose. She asked me to leave them alone, to let them wander about in peace. Of course, I didn't need much convincing. Without you, they were puppets with cut strings. I didn't have the heart to kill them."

Peter shifted uncomfortably. He didn't think of Hook as having that sort of honor.

"In any case, when she came to negotiate, we wound up talking for hours. Complaining about you, mostly. You were always the worst thorn in both our sides."

"Hey," Peter said, but it was halfhearted.

"She was a better card player than anyone in my crew," Hook said, "and made far more interesting conversation." He let out a shaky breath. "Damnation. Between the two of us, we've made quite a mess."

Cold was starting to seep into Peter's back from the cavern wall. He leaned forward, burying his face in his knees.

"Neverland's different," he mumbled. "It's not like it was when I was a boy. It's not—fun anymore."

"That's the trick of growing up. Nothing stays the same." Hook sounded oddly sympathetic. "You see the faults in everything. Including yourself."

Peter scrubbed at his eyes, thinking of how he had seen himself reflected in the Lost Boys' faces when they had betrayed him. They had been so afraid of him.

"I, for one, appreciate that you've become at least a little less whimsical," Hook said, in a lighter tone. "I don't know how I should have dealt with you if you came back still a child. All that nonsense about being the boy who couldn't grow up—I suppose that was just a joke of yours? Thank heavens."

Peter lifted his head to scowl at him. To his surprise, Hook smiled wearily back, smoke blooming from between his lips.

"I suppose you never gave any thought to the adults who had to deal with your games," he said. "Imagine having a well-cultivated pirate crew and an established career as the terror of the seas, only to have some bloody ten-year-old show up claiming he's the spirit of youth and joy and your unholy nemesis. Oh, and he's rallied a bunch of other little boys to come and kill you."

"Serves you right for being a pirate," Peter said.

"I was never so much a pirate as when you started insisting we were mortal enemies," Hook said. "Before that, I hardly ever thought of myself as a villain. I was barely vicious."

"Oh, so it's *my* fault you're awful."

"I'm only saying that the story seemed to demand it, and I suspect it was your story." Hook sighed, settling against the cave wall. His voice grew stronger as he went on; talking seemed to comfort him. "It used to be my story, you know, when I was a boy and I had Neverland to myself. But then you came along, and you were so ruthless and insistent, before I knew it you'd snatched the narrative away from me. You claimed—you *insisted*—that it was you who cut off my hand, when it was perfectly clear that I had not had the hand well before you arrived. You then told me you had fed the hand to a crocodile who would follow me to the ends of the earth, and lo and behold, such a crocodile appeared and hunted me until its death. The very world here bends for the sake of your stories, Pan. I see no reason why I, a mere man, should not."

That was not at all how Peter remembered it—but he also could not remember cutting off Hook's hand. He swallowed, sure that Hook was lying.

"You're the one who followed me up the mountain," he said. "You tried to feed me to the crocodiles. *You* killed Slightly. I didn't make you do any of that."

"I'll admit it was a collaborative effort," Hook said. "But you wanted a war."

That it was so unfair it set Peter's teeth on edge. "I didn't *want* Tink to die," he snapped. "I didn't want anyone to get *really* hurt."

"Or you didn't want it to be your responsibility," Hook said. "You didn't want it to be anyone you cared about. You wanted me to be at fault for every unpleasant part of it, while you played the bereaved hero seeking revenge for his losses, is that right?"

Peter opened his mouth and then snapped it shut, so incensed he could hardly speak. The worst part was that it was true. The truth of it punctured his anger like a pin in a balloon, and the tide of disgust and rage he'd directed at Hook turned grimly back toward himself.

"For what it's worth, I don't blame you." Hook chuckled around his cigar. "It would be difficult to be you without an opponent, wouldn't it?"

"But I didn't want anyone to die," Peter said, his throat tight. "I *didn't*."

"You killed my pirates," Hook said. "Don't tell me they provoked you."

Peter remembered with a flash of guilt how eagerly he had attacked Hook's helpless men on the shore. It had felt so innocent then, like playing with dolls. Looking back, he felt sick. "I didn't want to," he repeated. "I thought I did, but I wish I hadn't. I wish they were all still here, even if we were fighting. Slightly—Samuel—*Tink*—"

His throat closed around her name and tears stung the corners of his eyes, and he was too miserable to be ashamed of crying in front of Hook.

There was a long quiet. Then Hook said almost gently, "Cheer up, Pan. We'll plant their ashes and grow a new crop, and next time you can do things differently."

"What—what are you talking about?"

"You'll imagine yourself a few new orphans from Kensington and I'll pick up a few new rogues off a shipwreck, and between us we'll have two armies worth pitting against each other again... or leaving to their own devices while we keep the war between us.

Whatever you like."

Peter had the feeling that Hook was trying to comfort him. "You're not making any sense."

"They're *toys*, Pan. I hate to see you weeping over them as if they were real."

A strange chill ran down Peter's spine. "What?"

Hook blinked slowly. "Hadn't you ever realized? It's just you and I, Pan. Those boys of yours are toy soldiers."

"That's not true," Peter said, his heart thumping, "that's *horrible*, they're not—"

He stopped.

He remembered coming to Neverland as a boy and, finding himself alone and outnumbered by pirates, wishing for playmates. He had wanted boys like his brothers, a little younger than him, who would look up to him and follow his orders. One by one, such children had appeared, until he was finding a new Lost Boy every time he turned a corner in the woods. And as soon as the hideout had started to grow cramped, they had stopped coming.

As if his wish had been summoning them. Or creating them.

Hook was watching him, a frown digging into his brow. "You didn't know."

"I thought—" Peter could hardly shape the words, his lips trembling with disbelief. "I thought they were real," he whispered.

"Well, they are as real as Neverland can make them, but—good God, Pan, no wonder you've been so upset."

Peter drew a sharp breath. "What about the pirates?"

"My inventions, not yours."

The question he really wanted to ask caught in his throat for a long moment before he could voice it: "What about you? Are you...?"

Hook gave a startled scoff. "Me? I was here long before you, and I plan to be here long after. Yes, I'm *real*." There was a faint gleam in his eye. "You didn't think you invented me, did you?"

Peter realized he had been terrified of that, terrified that Hook too could be swept away from him with a thought. But if it was at least the two of them... He took a deep breath, feeling adrift but less afraid than he had been a moment ago.

"And Samuel?"

Hook faltered. "What do you think?" Before Peter could venture a guess, he gave a sharp little laugh and looked away. "He was a dream. Someone to warm my bed where it was safe to imagine such things."

Even if Samuel weren't real, Hook's grief was, and it twisted at him. "I'm sorry."

"It's all right," Hook said. "It doesn't pay to take things so seriously here, Pan."

He sounded like he wanted to put the memories away and forget them, and Peter couldn't blame him for that.

In the gloom, he could not see much of Hook's face, but there was clarity in that. The contrast of shadow and firelight peeled away his wild hair, his pirate coat, and even the hook itself. It left a man with a careful, aloof expression, skeptical eyebrows and a sardonic smile that came often and easily. He could almost be ordinary.

"Who are you?" Peter thought to ask.

Hook did not seem to notice that this was the first time Peter had ever wondered. He replied unhelpfully,

"James Hook, captain of the *Jolly Roger*."

"Is that really your name?"

"As far as I'm concerned." Hook laughed to himself. "I don't recall my old surname, but Hook suits me. I've been here long enough that it doesn't matter. Can you imagine going back to boring, ordinary life once you've experienced this place? Well, I suppose you have—and I did too, long ago. But wherever I came from, it paled in comparison to this place, so I decided to stay."

Peter hunched his shoulders. He didn't know where Hook came from, but he knew that for himself, the real world wasn't boring—it was something worse than that.

Hook was contemplating him again when Peter looked up. "We'd best move on," he said. "Your time is short."

Eight

"As the fearsome Hook prepared to send his helpless victim off the plank, he had no idea who was watching from above." Peter stretched one foot across the divide between two tree branches. Below, John snarled convincingly and menaced Michael with a sharpened stick, pushing him toward the end of a wooden board laid across the ground. Peter kept one eye on his brothers, but looking down made him nervous, so he focused on climbing around to the branches above them. "Little did Hook know that Peter Pan was preparing a daring rescue! When all hope seemed lost for Hook's prisoner, he heard..." Peter cleared his throat and called out in his clearest, most confident voice: "*Hook! If you feed that boy to the crocodiles, I'll cut you to ribbons!*"

John whirled around, feigning shock. "Who is that? Where's that coming from?"

"*'Tis I,*" Peter shouted, "*your mortal enemy, Peter Pa—*"

The branch broke under Peter's heel as he stepped forward to give the rest of his speech. He caught a glimpse of John's face, which sported a look of comical horror, before he slammed into the ground.

His wrist, which had been between him and the dirt, exploded in pain when he tried to use it to push himself up. "*Ow,*" Peter cried, rolling onto his back and clutching his arm to his chest.

"Wendy, are you broken?" Michael exclaimed, wandering off the plank to stare down at him.

"Let me see," John said importantly, crouching down and pushing his glasses up his nose. He spent a few minutes poking and prodding at Peter's arm to determine if it was broken. "You might lose the limb," he reported.

Peter was more upset that this meant the game was over, and that it might mean he wasn't allowed to play in the tree anymore. Mrs. Darling had made threats over his various bruises and scrapes before, but his arm seemed more serious. Still, it hurt too much to ignore. It was an awful pain, growing as his brothers picked him up and dragged him inside. And it wasn't only his arm—it was his whole body. His chest ached, raw as a cough, hot as a furnace, throbbing like a fever...

~~*

"Pan! *Pan!*"

Peter dragged himself from a deep, dark place.

He was sweating so much he felt as if he had melted, and his body was shaking violently. He could feel his bones trembling against the floor. A thumb and forefinger pulled one of his eyes open, and a face swam into view above him, but he could not make sense of it. He tried to speak, but words eluded him; he gasped like a drowning man.

His chest was on fire, all of it, centered around a singular searing pain. Hook touched the skin near the wound and Peter sobbed and thrashed at him, too weak to fight. "God damn and hellfire," Hook hissed. "I thought you had more time."

It took all Peter's strength to stay conscious, the cave blurring around Hook's face.

"Nothing for it," Hook said. He took Peter's chin and pried his mouth open. Peter tried instinctively to bite as Hook fit something between his teeth and forced his head back.

A vile liquid slid down his throat and he swallowed convulsively, tasting its bitterness all the way to his stomach.

"What," he managed to croak.

"The antidote," Hook said. "You idiot," he added for good measure.

He almost needn't have spoken. Peter could feel the substance spreading through his body; it was as quick as the poison had been, a silvery frost that seemed to snuff the fire in his blood. The fever receded so fast he was still gasping from the heat when it was suddenly gone. It left a potent exhaustion in its wake, black spots dancing in front of his eyes and threatening to swallow his vision.

What he could see was that Hook was very close to him, frowning. His fingers slid through Peter's damp bangs and pushed them away from his brow, and Peter's breath shook in his chest. He could smell the cigar Hook had smoked earlier. He made a startled noise of protest as Hook slid an arm around his shoulders, lifting him away from the wall. The heat of his body made Peter realize how cold he was in comparison. Working awkwardly with his one hand, Hook wrapped something warm and thick around Peter before setting him back against the wall.

Peter stared blankly at the shiny blue velvet for a long moment before he realized he was wearing Hook's coat.

"Better?" Hook asked.

"Don't touch me," Peter said thickly. He didn't like the feeling of his body warming to match Hook's; it made his skin crawl, like the shiver of electricity. He couldn't make sense of it with his head spinning, his limbs so heavy and weak.

Hook gave him a strange look from under his eyelashes and rose, stepping back. Peter lolled his head to the side to watch him, but that made him dizzy, and the world soon faded to black again.

~~*

"Mother!" John bellowed. "Come quickly! Wendy's hurt!"

They burst into the parlor and froze when they found it full of more grown-ups than usual. There was Mrs. Darling, as expected, but she was pouring tea for Mr. Darling, who ought to have been at work, and a stuffy-looking gentleman with a severe mustache.

"What's all this?" the gentleman asked. At a glance, Peter could see that he was the kind of grown-up who did not like children.

Mr. Darling looked mortified. "My—my children," he said. "You three, what on earth is this about?" He was staring at Peter with a kind of growing anger, his face turning pink.

"Wendy fell out of a tree and broke her arm," John said, standing up straight as a soldier.

The stuffy gentleman had glasses like John's, and he adjusted them as he bent forward. "Goodness," he said. "Is that your daughter?"

Mr. Darling's face turned an even deeper shade of red, and he shot Peter a venomous look. "It's a game she likes to play," he snapped. "Mary—"

Mrs. Darling was already sweeping forward in a swirl of skirts, rushing all three children upstairs. She sent John and Michael off to the nursery and pulled Peter into the washroom.

"Mother?" Peter hated crying, but he was on the brink of it, swallowing and trying to force the tears back. He didn't care about the pain of his arm, only the look on Mr. Darling's face. "Why's Father mad at me?"

Mrs. Darling was busy scrubbing the dirt from his cheeks. "He's not mad at you, dear," she said, which was what she always said, and Peter didn't believe her. "Your father is entertaining a very important man from the bank and wants to present the best picture of his family, that's all."

"What does that mean?" Peter asked, screwing up his face. Mrs. Darling tutted and began scrubbing at the dirt on his arms instead. "I'm not the best picture of his family?"

"Dear heart," Mrs. Darling said in the soothing way that always made Peter feel worse. "When you've grown up a bit more, you'll understand. The way you play with your brothers is very sweet, but you let them get you into all sorts of trouble. Now, when your father wants someone to see the best picture of his family, he wants to see you behaving like a young lady, not like Michael and John."

"But I don't want to."

Mrs. Darling didn't seem to hear him. "Right now your father is probably feeling embarrassed because Mr. Martin saw his daughter dressed as a boy. So why don't we get you dressed up in your prettiest frock and you can go downstairs and introduce yourself to Mr. Martin properly? I think that would make your papa feel much better."

The very idea of parading in front of his father and a strange man in a pretty frock made Peter's skin crawl. "My arm's broken," he cried. "I can't go downstairs."

"It's not broken, dearest; you've been moving it. I'm sure it's just sprained." Mrs. Darling smiled, as sweet as always, but there was something unmoving in her eyes. "We'll visit the doctor to be sure once Mr. Martin has gone home."

There was nothing for it. Peter let himself be cleaned up, had his hair brushed out and safely contained in ribbons, and was marched down to the living room in a blue silk dress with his aching right arm dangling at his side as if it didn't hurt. "George, dear?" Mrs. Darling called, in her honeyed voice. "Wendy's coming down to say hello to Mr. Martin."

Mr. Darling looked braced for impact when Peter and Mrs. Darling came into the parlor, but when he saw Peter in his dress, he abruptly relaxed. His smile softened as if he had recognized someone he cared about in a stranger's face.

"There's my young lady," he said gruffly. "There's my beautiful girl."

Nine

Pan was scowling in his sleep when Hook returned to their makeshift camp. Hook looked enviously at him—Pan was still bundled in his coat, and Hook hadn't the heart to take it back, which meant *he* was wearing only his blood-soaked shirt and slowly freezing to death.

His scouting had failed to provide him with any additional sources of light, warmth, food, or indeed anything but pale tunnels and a lot of uncomfortably sharp stalagmites. They were thoroughly trapped, without resources, and the stab wound Pan had inflicted on his shoulder was growing more painful by the hour.

Hook hunkered down beside the aforementioned devil. Pan was a different creature when he was asleep; the cleverness and cruelty smoothed out of his face, leaving behind a young man who could almost be mundane. That was the trick of him, of course. His magic was all in the way he moved, like he had a mastery over the world which entitled him to bend its rules.

In sleep, however, he was obviously human, especially while pale and curled up inside a coat many sizes too large for him. Hook didn't like it, much as he should perhaps have enjoyed seeing Pan brought low; it felt wrong to see him helpless. It plucked at sympathies Hook had almost forgotten he had.

Knowing that Pan had been playing their game unwittingly, thinking that the stakes were truly life and death for his Lost Boys, made Hook feel all the worse for him.

"Hurry up and feel better," he said. He wasn't expecting a reply, but Pan shifted in his sleep, groaning something indistinct.

Hook frowned. Pan's face was twisted up in distress, his jaw clenched. Concerned that he might still be feverish, Hook felt his forehead.

At his touch, Pan's eyes fluttered open and he gasped.

Hook snatched his hand back, half expecting to be bitten for his trouble. Pan had felt quite cold, no trace of the poison fever remaining, but he looked disoriented. His sharp green eyes darted around as if he were not quite sure where he was, and then fixed on Hook.

"My apologies," Hook said. "I meant to let you sleep for as long as you could."

"It's fine," Pan said hoarsely.

"You look more like the living than you did. How are you feeling?"

"Fine." Pan pulled Hook's coat tighter around his thin shoulders. He didn't look well.

"Perhaps I should have clarified. Are you still about to succumb to the poison, or can we take that particular worry off our plates?"

Pan's brow wrinkled. "I feel better," he said in a tone of slight suspicion. "You gave me the antidote. Why?"

"Because I fell asleep on watch and woke to find you dying." Hook said it lightly, not allowing his tone to give away how alarming it had been to hear Pan crying out in his sleep, to discover him sweating and shaking. It had occurred to Hook that if something had gone wrong—if the vial of antidote had been cracked in their struggles—Pan would be gone, and it would be his fault.

Really, that was an outcome he ought to have been content with. Wasn't it Pan's job to survive all Hook's attempts to kill him?

Then again, whose fault it was made little difference if, in the end, Pan was suffering and Hook didn't want him to.

Pan looked as conflicted as Hook felt. "Where would be the fun in you expiring now?" Hook asked him. "Do you think I'd really rather spend the rest of my short life wandering these caves alone?"

"No," Pan admitted. "That sounds boring."

"Boring and probably fatal. A dreadful combination."

Pan almost smiled. Hook saw him stop halfway and scowl instead. There was still something tense and uncertain hanging around him, something in his face like an echo of pain. It was probably not in Hook's best interests to pry, and yet...

"You looked like you were having an unhappy sleep," he said. "Were you dreaming?"

Pan hunched his shoulders. That was it; Hook saw the crack in his expression. Pan wrapped his arms around his knees in that defensive way he had. "Yes," he said shortly, clearly not intending to elaborate.

"Tell me," Hook said. He raised his eyebrows when Pan glared at him. "Why not?"

"You'd use it against me," Pan said.

"Give me some credit. I've done a fine job of terrorizing you thus far without access to your nightmares."

"That doesn't mean you wouldn't," Pan said, though rather halfheartedly.

"I find that enemies are the most satisfying people to share secrets with," Hook said. "If you must tell someone, tell someone who's sensitive to all your vulnerabilities, on account of trying to exploit them."

"That doesn't make sense."

"I'm making excuses for you," Hook said impatiently. "You seem like the type to bottle up without an excuse. Talk to me or not; the choice is yours."

Pan's ears turned pink. He stared at the floor. "I was dreaming about my father," he said abruptly.

"Ah. Dead?"

"No."

"Mine is," Hook said. "My mother as well."

"Oh," Pan said, looking vaguely chagrined. "Sorry."

"There's no need to be. They died when I was small. The only relatives I had left, in fact, were the ones who barely knew my parents, and they shuffled me around constantly, each of them hoping that one of the *other* relatives would like me enough to adopt me permanently." It was a very old memory, and it had lost almost all its sting. "There, you've a secret of mine. Tell me one of yours."

"My father didn't love me," Pan said. "Nobody did."

Hook paused, startled not only by the sentiment itself—it had never occurred to him that Pan could be unloved—but by the way he said it. There was no doubt or hope for reassurance in Pan's words, only bruising certainty.

"They all wanted me to be someone else," Pan

continued. "But I wasn't. So they didn't want me."

"So you ran away to Neverland," Hook said, and Pan gave a stiff nod. "But they still torment you in dreams."

"They don't mean to," Pan said, his voice fading a little. "They just do."

"It'll get better. I used to have dreams like that needling at me every hour I spent here. But they do go away with time—as a matter of fact, I couldn't tell you what I used to dream about." Hook laughed through the uncomfortable thought that he had probably forgotten terrible things that now lay out of reach of his mind.

Pan, meanwhile, looked somewhat reassured. "You think they'll be gone someday?"

"I'm sure of it." Hook caught his eye. "And as for your other fears... I may be rather dastardly, but there are things even I wouldn't stoop to use against you. Honor among thieves, you know."

Pan bit his lip, flickers of that boyish vulnerability in his face. Hook didn't know how to comfort him except to move on. "Speaking of honor," he said, "you now owe me for saving your life—so if you've rested enough, I suggest you get back to work on finding us a way out of here."

That did the trick. Pan frowned and climbed to his feet. If he was still weak, he did his best to avoid showing it as he fumbled his way out of Hook's coat.

"We need water," Hook added. "And something to eat, soon. I scouted ahead while you were asleep—this passage caves in as well. Have you any ideas?"

Pan shook his head. "You made it sound like we were gods," he said slowly. "Why don't we just make a way out?"

"Come, now," Hook said. "That's hardly the spirit of the thing."

~~*

They soon faced another bitter reality: Hook was running out of matches. The hardwood burned for a long time, but he didn't think two sticks would give them more than another few hours, and then they would be traveling blind.

"It doesn't seem fair," he said amiably as they walked. "I've lived a good life. I've killed and plundered so many of my enemies, amassed so much power, and when it comes down to it, I'm going to die alone in a cave with *you*."

"You make it sound like you're the one getting the short end of the bargain," Pan snipped back. He was almost back to his usual self, though something in his manner was subdued. His edges had softened.

For his part, Hook found he couldn't muster his usual vinegar either, though that was mostly to do with his increasing exhaustion. His shoulder, where Pan had stabbed him, was developing a new kind of pain, a stinging, needle-like sensation that was far harder to ignore than its previous dull ache. He had gotten along so far by hoping that it wouldn't trouble him until he was outside. But now the wound was hot; he could feel it radiating a sickly warmth against the inside of his shirt.

That was probably a bad sign.

"Would you mind giving me some of your energy?" he asked, when it became obvious that Pan was slowing down to allow him to keep up. "Hell's teeth, I'm hungry."

"There must be something to eat down here," Pan said. "We might even be able to fish if we find an opening to the sea."

"Oh, what a wonderful idea. I'm sure the kraken would appreciate another chance at devouring us."

"*I'll* go fishing, then," Pan said. "You can hide around the corner if you like."

Hook sniffed. "If you can procure us a fish, I'll see about cooking it."

"Who knew you were such a coward?"

"It's not fear, it's pragmatism. One of us can fly; the other is wounded."

Pan glanced at him, but let the topic go surprisingly easily. Hook waited for more jibes, but the next thing out of Pan's mouth was, "Is your shoulder hurting you?"

It was said in a tone of slight condescension, as if Pan would never have deigned to be hurt, but it was unmistakably an expression of concern. Hook almost smiled. "Don't start worrying about me now, or you'll be devastated to realize how many times you've tried to kill me before."

"I owe you," Pan said defensively. "I don't care if you die after I pay you back."

"Rest assured that I have no plans to die either before or after."

"We'll see about that." It probably would have been threatening, except that there was no bite in Pan's voice. Maybe he was tired too; it wouldn't have surprised Hook if Pan's careless demeanor was meant to throw him off the scent.

Well, Hook couldn't exactly fault him for that. Here he was growing wearier with every step yet doing his best to seem unaffected. He was afraid of Pan doing something chivalrous like offering to help him walk, and he couldn't imagine anything more embarrassing than having to lean on that young stick insect for support.

The cave floor sloped down for a while, a damp and slippery decline that made it hard to keep their footing. Difficult for Hook, at least. Pan walked lightly, practically treading on air. Hook felt his way along the wall, trying to ignore the feeling that he was inevitably going to fall and die.

It was almost a relief when his foot finally did catch on something, sending him sailing forward.

Pan lunged caught him by the collar, stumbling to a halt with Hook tangled in his arms. "What was that?" Hook said, trying to turn around while Pan hastily released him.

"You tripped," Pan said accusingly.

"No, something tripped me." Hook picked up the match he'd dropped and edged up the slope. "There, look."

There was a shallow stone slab set into the floor with a lip high enough for someone's shoe to snag on. "What's that?" Pan asked.

Before Hook could even guess, Pan—the unbelievable fool—leaned over and pressed his palm to the slab.

"Pan, *don't*—"

At the press of Pan's hand, the slab sank down into the floor, and there was a deep grinding sound like stone being carved. Hook looked up in time to see an enormous boulder crashing through the ceiling and rolling down toward them. It was wide enough to fill the tunnel, with no avenue for escape.

He seized Peter by the back of the shirt and yanked

him down the passage, roaring, "*Run!*"

There was no chance they would make it. They sprinted and slid wildly down the slope, barely staying on their feet, but the boulder gained second by second. There was no sign of an end to the slope. The matchstick in Hook's hand blew out, but in the moment before the light vanished, he saw a shallow alcove in the wall.

Pan must have seen it at the same time. With the boulder just behind their heels, he spun and threw himself bodily against Hook, smashing them both into the alcove. The impact went through Hook's wounded shoulder like a fresh blade and he gasped, his vision spotting.

When he came back to himself, he was breathing hard, and Pan was pressed into him. The boulder was crashing away down the passage. Hook felt the heat of Pan's breath on his cheek and his body, quite of its own accord, began to document the places where they were touching.

Pan jerked back. Hook followed him from the alcove and lit his final match, grimacing as his shoulder throbbed. In the sudden light, Pan looked flushed and guilty.

"Your shoulder," he began. "I'm sorry—I didn't mean to..."

"It's all right. You saved both our lives." Pan looked even more awkward at that. "It seems we're not meant to be here," Hook added. "Which is a good sign. Shall we?"

There was a cavern at the bottom of the slope, larger than any they had stepped into before. The walls spread out far enough in both directions that it was impossible to determine their limits. Hook stopped in the doorway, unnerved by the vastness of it. Pan walked on, tipping his head up curiously.

Hook followed his gaze and gasped. The roof of the enormous cavern was made of crystal, like the interior of a geode; the matchlight twinkled across it, a series of blinking stars in the dark.

It was a moment before Hook realized why there was excitement building in his chest.

"I know where we are," he said.

Ten

Peter spun around to see Hook staring up at the glittering ceiling, transfixed with wonder. "Where?" Peter demanded. "Can you find us a way out?"

"Maybe," Hook breathed. "I tried to find this place for *years*. The dread pirate Red Dog laid his hoard of treasure to rest in the crystal caves below the island, according to his old cabin boy. We hunted and hunted, but never managed to find the entrance. All the wealth he amassed over a lifetime of piracy is supposed to be kept hidden in this place."

Peter's excitement faded. "If you've never been here before… doesn't that mean we're even more lost?"

Hook waved him off. "That's not the point."

"That *is* the point. Treasure's all very well, but I'm starving."

"We'll find something to eat," Hook said. He took a further step into the cavern, matchlight weaving as he swung it out to illuminate more of the cave. He winced when he moved his arm but barely seemed aware of it, his eyes shining. "Don't you understand? All the riches you've ever seen pale in comparison to Red Dog's wealth, Pan, and we've stumbled upon it by accident. It must be fate."

He grinned, and in spite of himself, Peter felt a reluctant grin creeping onto his face in return. He had never seen Hook so purely excited; there was something almost youthful about him as he gazed up at the sparkling ceiling.

Peter was still uncomfortably conscious of how badly he had jarred Hook's wounded shoulder, and Hook's visible pallor made it hard to believe he was as lively as he sounded. "Are you sure you don't need a rest?"

"When did you get so thoughtful?" Hook asked. "Come on. There's supposed to be five entrances to the large cave—four, excluding the one we came in—and a carving somewhere that indicates the passage leading to the treasure."

He set off before Peter could protest. Peter followed him, rubbing his arms in the cold. "What if he hid his fortunes in a different crystal cave?"

"Shut up and help me look." Hook glanced over his shoulder, a smirk curling the corner of his mouth. "If you must know, finding the treasure will find us the way out. Red Dog's cabin boy said there was a secret passage leading directly to the treasure room—and that it could be found somewhere in the forest."

Peter quickened his pace, his heart leaping. "Why didn't you say so?"

"Because I enjoy listening to you complain like a petulant child."

Peter considered kicking him.

The crystal cavern was so large it took them at least half an hour of walking along one wall to discover a second passage leading out. Hook crouched on the floor and studied it for any sign of a symbol that would indicate it lead to the treasure room, but was unsatisfied, so they continued.

They repeated this process several times over, and Peter started to feel uneasily that the cave might go on forever. When they reached the fifth passage, which had caved in and was equally unmarked, even Hook began to look a little crestfallen. The remaining color had drained from his face as they walked. It was hard to tell whether they had circled all the way around to where they had come in.

"Why don't we try going down the other passages?" Peter asked.

"I suppose we may have to," Hook said. "But the other entrances were supposed to be trapped as well."

"I can handle traps."

"I know you're prepared to fight your way through anything, but there is something to be said for thinking before you sprint off into danger," Hook retorted. "We don't know how long any of the tunnels are. They might go for miles in the wrong direction, and we've hardly any light left."

"Fine. So how do we figure out which is the right one?"

Hook didn't answer. He was looking haggard. He rubbed at his chin, where the beard was getting overgrown. "I don't know," he admitted. "Do you think those mushrooms are poisonous?"

Peter followed his gaze to the clusters of white mushrooms growing along the wall. "I think I've seen Ernest pick these," he said, crouching. He was a little doubtful, but the fringed cap on the mushrooms looked identical. He plucked one, studied it briefly, and popped it into his mouth.

"Good Lord," Hook said. "There's no more antidote, you know."

Peter chewed. The mushroom had a flaky texture and tasted nutty, and to his empty stomach, it was delicious. "I think they're fine."

"You would think so. I'll wait and see if you keel over, thank you."

Peter shrugged and picked a few more. After a resentful pause, Hook sighed and squatted beside him, picking a few mushrooms of his own.

"If you keel over, I'll die anyway," he muttered. "I may as well die with a full stomach."

He sank fully to the floor, nibbling on the mushrooms. It was hard to tell in the low light, but his skin looked shiny. Peter stopped himself from reaching out and feeling Hook's forehead; he was afraid of finding it feverish.

"Your shoulder—" he began.

"I'm trying not to think about it," Hook said.

Peter took a nervous breath. "Let me see it," he said. "You need to sit down for a while anyway."

"I can't stand this new conscientiousness of yours," Hook said, but without feeling. He looked wretched.

Peter took the match, crouching in front of him as Hook removed his coat.

His heart clenched. Hook's white shirt was soaked in drying blood from the left shoulder down to the breast. Beneath the torn shirt, Peter could see the outline of the gash his knife had made. It was bleeding sluggishly still, probably because Peter had slammed him against a wall. It was not particularly deep, yet it was angry and swollen, blackened blood welling from the wound.

Their eyes caught. "I've had worse," Hook said.

"You should have bandaged it," Peter said. "Why didn't you?"

"For one thing, I don't have a bandage. For another, why didn't I secure a bandage around my shoulder by matchlight with one hand and a hook?"

Hook arched his eyebrows. "I wonder."

"You could have asked me to do it."

"Could I have?"

"*Yes*." Peter felt a spike of anger; he wanted Hook to trust him. "We're working together, remember? And I owe you."

A little smirk curled the corner of Hook's mouth. "Indeed," he said. "Well, have at it."

His movements were stiff as he began to peel off his shirt. Peter moved in to help him when it became obvious that he was struggling to lift his injured arm above his head, and snagging the cloth on his claw. Hook's shirt was fine, silky linen, and warm in Peter's hands.

It somehow hadn't occurred to Peter that this step, undressing Hook, would be necessary. He was suddenly full of nerves, his stomach doing flips. He almost wanted to take his offer back, but he could hardly do that. It wasn't that he didn't want to touch Hook, exactly—he did, if only because dressing the wound would feel a little like undoing the damage he'd done.

He let the match smolder on the floor beside Hook's knee, its faint light wavering over them both. It was bright enough for Peter to make out more than the wound. He tore his eyes quickly away from the dark hair that scattered across Hook's chest and down his belly, although it looked soft enough to touch.

"I can't believe I'm letting you near an open wound," Hook said lightly. "I've seen the squalor you and your Lost Boys live in."

"Shut up." Even Peter could see that there wasn't exactly a hygienic solution. He'd have to focus on the bleeding for now and worry about everything else later.

For lack of other materials, he took a sleeve from Hook's shirt and tore it into a long strip. Hook gasped in protest, but Peter ignored him.

The Lost Boys had gotten into all kinds of perilous situations, and had to work with makeshift bandages to heal many wounds. Peter was used to that. He wasn't used to the unusual heat that Hook's skin seemed to radiate, or to the way he felt himself flushing as if in response as he edged close enough to wind the bandage over Hook's shoulder. His fingers brushed across the upper curve of Hook's arm, and Peter jumped.

He's real, he thought.

He pulled the bandage tight, and Hook gave a muted groan from behind clenched teeth. "Sorry," Peter said.

"It's all right," Hook said. "I'd rather be down here and wounded than... not." It didn't sound like he'd meant to say *not*, but rather trailed off from something weightier. Peter glanced at him and didn't know what to make of Hook's expression. He was watching Peter's hands as he tied off the bandage.

"Why?" Peter asked.

"Why would I rather be stuck underground with the wretched youth who's been trying to kill me since his return to Neverland, rather than being free and whole in the world outside?"

"Yes."

Hook looked abashed. "Well, for all that went wrong, it's been quite a lot more exciting since you came back."

"It *was* fun," Peter found himself saying. "When it was just the two of us fighting."

"Yes, it was, wasn't it?" Hook caught his eye, and Peter backed away from a feeling he didn't understand. He sat on the ground, watching Hook shift and lean against the cave wall with a wince.

The tattered remains of Hook's shirt lay on the ground between them.

"It's awfully cold," Hook said.

"I wish we could make a fire," Peter said. "It'd be hard to cook a fish even if I found one."

"I have flint in one of these pockets," Hook said. "I didn't anticipate being somewhere without any wood."

"I'll look for something flammable," Peter said, getting to his feet. "Maybe that pirate captain left something." Mostly he didn't want to sit there and think about the moment they'd shared. He leaned forward to take the match from Hook. "You should rest."

"I'll sing," Hook said, "in case you have trouble finding your way back."

Peter set off with Hook's low voice humming away behind him.

For a while he kept to the chamber's edge, feeling his way along the wall and finding nothing. Then it occurred to him that there was a whole vast unexplored space in the center of the cavern, where they had not really ventured. Already Hook sounded far away, yet Peter hadn't even stepped out from the wall.

Peter turned toward the blackness and started out, and immediately knew why they hadn't done so before. It was deeply unpleasant to walk away from the wall into the dark; the cavern was empty, nothing but cold slippery stone and starry crystal above. It felt like walking across a frozen sea at night. The fading of Hook's singing behind him only made him more unsettled, and he found himself straining his ears to try to hear it better. There was no other sound.

Then, ahead, he saw huge, skeletal fingers stretching toward him. Peter crept slowly forward and the fingers became bare black tree branches.

The tree was enormous. It stretched up toward the glittering ceiling, and might have touched it; it went too high to see. It was dead, and dry as bone. Its trunk was perforated with snaking tunnels, as if it had been eaten from the inside out.

As Peter approached, he stumbled over something that rolled away with a clatter. Looking down, he saw the ground littered with broken branches.

~~*

"Where on earth did you find that?" Hook exclaimed, as Peter dumped a pile of wood on the ground beside him.

Peter took the flint from him and began striking sparks into the pile of kindling. The dry branches lit easily, smoking and then sprouting small orange flames like fungus. Soon they had a fire blazing, heat washing over them.

Hook startled when Peter told him of the dead tree. "A fairy commune. Of course."

"Of course?"

"Red Dog was obsessed with fairies. He devoted his life to studying them, when he wasn't playing pirate. He naturally would have chosen a hiding place for his treasure that had something to do with the fae." Hook gazed thoughtfully at the crystal high above them. "I suppose these caves must have been a gathering place for them, once."

The spark was back in his eyes. He smiled at the look on Peter's face. "This is the kind of thing that enchanted me as a child," he said. "Buried treasure, lost fortunes, mystic places…"

Peter tried to picture Hook as a little boy exploring caverns like these, pretending to be a dread pirate. It was funny, but it made him feel odd. He hadn't realized they had so much in common.

"Even if we find the treasure, you're not going to be able to carry much gold out of here, you know," he said.

"I'll see to it that we mark the entrance so I can return and claim the lot of it," Hook said. "And not all treasure is gold and jewels."

That caught Peter's attention. "It's not gold?"

Hook sighed, a little dreamily. "Oh, he had the requisite fortunes. Vast quantities of stolen riches, heaps of diamonds, mountains of pearls—everything you could dream of. But he also had a coat made of spider silk that took a million spiders to spin, and a pair of merskin boots said to be made from the freely given scales of a mer queen. A wardrobe fit for a god. *That* was his real treasure."

Peter stared at him. "Are you serious?"

"Why wouldn't I be?"

Peter didn't know how to answer, except: "Did he really leave his clothes with his fortunes?"

"I bloody hope so," Hook said. "I certainly never found those boots anywhere else I looked."

Eleven

Despite the fire, it was cold—but when Hook woke, he found himself uncomfortably warm.

He had slept for a long time, drifting in and out of consciousness, the fading glow of the embers the only way by which he could tell time. They were in total darkness when at last he was fully awake. He only knew Pan was still there because he had stretched out one of his legs in his sleep and draped it across Hook's ankle.

Between the fever and his inability to see, it was hard to feel quite real. Hook nudged Pan with his foot until he heard an answering groan and levered himself into a sitting position. He couldn't put any weight on his injured shoulder; razors went through it when he tried, a sharp pain that burned for a long time afterward.

Pan managed to create a sort of torch out of a few white branches, although it would not burn long before it started eating at his fingers. When he lit it and saw Hook's face, he paled a little, concern obvious. "We've got to find a way out soon."

"I agree," Hook said, cradling his arm against his chest.

Pan took a deep breath. "Do you know anything else about Red Dog's treasure? Any other clues? What was the symbol he used to mark the right way out?"

"It was a fairy. I'd sketch it, but I haven't anything

to draw with."

"Why a fairy? Why did they interest him so much?"

"Red Dog was a private and mysterious man," Hook said. "A vicious brute, you understand, but he also wrote a lot of strange poetry. He was full of contradictions, and I've always believed he was as human as you and I, so perhaps he knew that the fae were more real than the other inhabitants of this place. He would sketch them in all their various forms—he was a bit of a naturalist as well as a pirate. I still have the book of sketches his cabin boy gave me."

Pan screwed up his face. He was not, as far as Hook could tell, a great fan of puzzles. "So... what does that tell us?"

"Nothing. I don't know anything else useful about the treasure or its location. Sylvester had never seen it—no one aside from Red Dog saw these caves and lived. He murdered every member of his crew who helped him carry the treasure to its resting place."

"Who's Sylvester?"

"The cabin boy," Hook said. "A fine man with a finer ass."

Pan spluttered. "What?"

"You heard me."

Pan seemed to have nothing to say to this. He leapt to his feet, leaving the torch, and stalked off abruptly into the shadows.

"Where are you going?" Hook heaved himself reluctantly to his feet. "Pan!"

"Sitting here won't help us," Pan shouted back. "Do you want to die in this cave?"

"Slow *down*," Hook said, going after him with the torch. He'd not taken Pan for the type to get upset over a mention of his attraction to men, least of all after he'd been so contrite over Samuel.

Nonetheless, it had apparently gotten under his skin, because Pan did not slow down. He walked too quickly for Hook to follow, and soon Hook was reduced to calling after him, having lost track of his shape in the dark. He was beginning to feel genuinely worried and more than a little angry when, in the distance, there was a flash of light.

"What was that?" Hook yelled.

For a moment, there was silence. Then Pan shouted back, high and startled, "I think I've found it!"

Hook hurried toward his voice, moving as quickly as he could. His body was weak and resisting and it seemed to take an age before the torchlight glanced off Peter's narrow form. He was standing beside the entrance to a tunnel.

Peter stretched out and touched the wall. Light flared where his palm met the stone. Approaching, Hook saw a rough sigil cut into the wall. It contained several skinny loops that might have been stylized fairy wings. "I just touched it," Peter said, his eyes wide. "I touched it and it lit up."

"That's it," Hook breathed. He reached out and stroked the sigil, but its light faded. "Why does it glow for you?"

"I don't know," Peter said, a little smugly. "Why doesn't it glow for you?"

He reached out to the wall again, and Hook saw the thin gash he had opened across his palm to summon the kraken.

"*Blood*," Hook said thoughtfully. "Like a sacrifice?"

He ran his fingers through the flaking blood on his shirt and pressed them to the sigil. Nothing happened, and Pan looked even smugger. "Just my blood, then," he said.

"Don't look so proud of yourself. I'm the one who cut your hand, so really..."

"I can't help it if I've saved us," Pan said. "Shall we go?"

Hook sniffed and peered down the tunnel. "Well, I have no guarantee that there aren't traps down this way as well, but it's the best chance we have. Well done."

They went into the corridor together, the air damp and stale within. There was no light, but a few meters in, there was another rough carving in the wall. When Pan touched it, the passage was bathed in a soft glow. The ceiling was made of jagged crystal which sparkled above them as they walked. Every so often there was a carving in the stone, so as one faded, they would reach the next without ever losing vision.

Hook was staring at the latest fairy sigil as they passed it, wondering, when it suddenly hit him.

"*Fairy dust*," he said, snapping his fingers.

"What?"

"It's in your blood," Hook said, pleased in spite of himself for having solved it. "That's why you can fly—Tinker Bell told me she gave you that gift."

She had, at times, expressed a certain regret for giving Pan that kind of power.

"So?" Pan asked.

"*So*," Hook said impatiently, "that's why the sigil reveals itself for you. It needed fairy dust, not blood. Ingenious, really. I never thought I'd need pixie dust to find the way to Red Dog's treasure."

Pan looked at his hand like he didn't quite recognize it. "She was always looking out for me," he said at length, and then fell quiet for a long time.

~~*

It was a good thing he had the merskin boots in mind as he continued, because Hook didn't know what else would have kept him walking.

The crystal passage went on for an eon, and as it did, Hook's fever worsened. He was beginning to have the unnerving feeling that he wasn't as concerned as he should have been; the fever wrapped him in a haze that was almost pleasant, dulling his thoughts.

He had survived worse, he told himself. Nothing in Neverland had ever managed to kill him before, so a little knife wound inflicted by Peter Pan wasn't going to do it either.

But his temperature continued to climb, even as Pan shivered and hunched his shoulders against the cold damp of the passage, and with each step Hook wasn't sure if he was about to float away or crumple to the floor.

When at last they reached the treasure room, he hardly noticed at first. It took Pan gasping and rushing ahead for him to realize that the latest twist in the passage looked different; he had been halfway asleep on his feet.

The treasure room itself was rather shabby. It was the only part of the caves that showed signs of having being shaped by human hands, aside from the trap in the tunnel. Shelves built into the walls were coated in years' worth of dust, and wooden support beams held up the ceiling. Glowing sigils lit the room at regular intervals, and in the center there was a mass of rusty chests.

On the other side, a small door was set into the rock. Pan put his shoulder against it, grunting as he shoved. "It's stuck," he said. "The kraken shaking everything up must have squashed it in. Give me a hand."

"Now, wait a minute," Hook said.

He was amazed to discover that the treasure chests were unlocked; apparently Red Dog had been confident enough in his traps that he hadn't felt the need for keys. The hinges, however, were rusted stiff. Hook pried open the first chest and found himself face-to-face with a small ocean of polished sapphires.

His mouth fell open. He dipped a hand into the chest, feeling the jewels' smooth edges slide over his fingers, and scooped up a handful.

"Pan, come over here."

Pan came obediently, although he looked exasperated. "You know where to find the cave now," he said. "There's no need to look at the treasure."

"I need a rest anyway," Hook insisted, partially because it was true—it was getting worryingly hard to keep his eyes open. "And I don't trust you not to collect your Lost Boys and raid the cave before I can get to it."

"I'd hold those boots for ransom," Peter said.

"Exactly. And speaking of boots, help me shift this chest."

Peter took most of the weight as they shunted the collection of sapphires to one side. Beneath it was a painted chest held shut by a dozen tiny clasps. "This looks special," Hook said, and set about undoing all the clasps. There was a gulp of air as the lid lifted, as if a seal had been broken.

A golden crown lay on top, set with sapphires and

emeralds. Each precious stone was wreathed with tiny blue and green pearls, and the largest sapphire was placed in the center of a stylized trident.

"Poseidon's circlet," Hook said, his heart pounding. "A crown for a sea king."

Pan snatched it. He danced out of arm's reach like he expected Hook to grab it back, and then placed it on his own head. "For the king of Neverland," he said.

"No one crowned you."

Pan grinned, the circlet slightly too large and slipping over one of his ears at a jaunty angle. "I don't need anyone to crown me," he said, unruffled. He picked up a polished silver platter from a nearby chest and studied his reflection in it, looking pleased by whatever he saw.

Hook scowled after him, resisting the words on the tip of his tongue. *It suits you*, he wanted to say, against all his better instincts. The crown made Pan look like a lazy young god, his curly hair spilling out under and over the golden rim. His eyes matched the jewels in their gleaming. *Prince of runaways*, Hook thought, and caught his breath and looked away.

He had an irritating notion that Pan didn't realize he was handsome, but Hook was going to reveal that to him by accident if he wasn't careful.

He refocused his attention on what the crown had been resting upon: a silk coat, pale gold, trimmed with black velvet. Hook ran his fingers over the fine stitching, scarcely daring to believe it. "There it is," he whispered. "Spider silk." He picked it up, holding it up in the matchlight, watching it shine. "Pan, *look*."

"I'm looking," Pan said.

"You must admit it's the most beautiful thing you've ever seen."

"You said we were telling stories," Pan said. "You didn't admit that the only story you wanted to tell was about clothes."

"Clothes, adventure, and a worthy opponent," Hook said, shooting him a look. "Who could ask for more?"

Pan turned pink and swiveled away, and Hook returned to digging through the chest. His fingers brushed over the texture of scales, and he lifted out the merskin boots with an involuntarily lustful sound. His shoulder throbbed when he lifted his arm, but Hook ignored it; the fever was helping to dampen the pain, making him drift. And anyway, the boots were knee-high and covered in blue-black scales, giving them a gloss like blackbird feathers.

They were beautiful, and they appeared to be his size. "God above," Hook said.

"We should go," Pan said. "You can't take the coat now, anyway, you'd bleed on it."

Hook dropped the boots back into the chest with a scowl. "Take that crown off, then. You can't bring it with you either."

He was almost sorry when Pan obeyed, laying Poseidon's circlet carelessly on a nearby chair. Then again, the most unfortunate thing of all was that taking off the crown didn't make him look any less regal. That was all in his bearing, in his arrogance and grace.

Standing up made Hook dizzy, but at least it gave him an excuse for feeling his stomach turn over as he approached Pan at the door. "Go on, then," he said. "Lead the way."

Twelve

The door did not go quietly. Peter bruised his arm trying to shove it, and in the end it took him and Hook pushing together until Hook's face turned gray to force the door open. They emerged behind a waterfall that cascaded into a shallow lake, showering the surrounding cliffs with mist. Sunlight flooded over them, streaming through the waterfall and dappling on the rocks.

It was a beautiful day. They were at the place where the mountains met the wildest forest, which was in full bloom.

"Here," Hook said. "There's a path around to shore." He began to pick his way tentatively across a narrow rocky ledge. He was still extremely pale; the strain of opening the door seemed to have taken the last of his strength. Peter flew along beside him, ready to catch him in case he slipped. When they reached the shore Hook sank to the ground abruptly, like his legs would not support him. When Peter moved closer to him, he could feel the heat radiating from his skin.

"What is it?" Peter asked, though he knew the answer.

"What do you think?" Hook asked between gritted teeth.

He struggled with his sleeves, trying to pull off his coat. Peter wrestled him free of it and pulled his tattered shirt over his head. Blood had soaked through the makeshift bandages on his shoulder, and they gave off a sharp, unpleasant smell. Peter unwound the bandages slowly, afraid of what he would find underneath. The wound was tender; Hook jerked and swallowed a curse when the cloth peeled away from it.

The gash itself didn't look markedly worse than before, but all around it the skin was inflamed, blotchy red with spidery dark veins extending out from the wound.

"Is it infected?" Peter asked helplessly. This would never have happened in the Neverland of his childhood.

"I should think so," Hook said. He looked down at the wound and then away, heaving a painful breath. A few beads of sweat rolled down his chest.

"What do I do?"

Hook flashed an anxious grin. "I don't suppose you have any more pixie dust up your sleeve," he said.

"No," Peter said. But a second later he lurched to his feet, leaving Hook on the ground. "Wait. Hold on!"

He sprinted off into the forest, crashing into the underbrush and tripping down the hill it had concealed. He caught himself in midair before he could hit the ground and scrambled on, half running, half flying.

He scanned the brush, the greenery tearing past him uninterrupted until—at last—he saw a familiar gleam of silver.

A fairy hive was wrapped in the boughs of a tree, swathed in papery gray silk. Peter seized the hive and shook it until the fairies came out, buzzing furiously and biting at his arms. "Stop it!" he cried. "It's me, Pan!"

Several more of the fairies bit him before they were satisfied. They were sluggish to follow even when he explained that he needed help, glaring at him with angry yellow eyes. He shouted until they came streaming after him, a procession of seven, all of them with shining black fur and sheet-glass wings.

Hook had slumped over when they returned, and for a moment Peter's heart stopped; he was irrationally afraid that Hook had managed to die in his absence. But when they saw Hook, the seven fairies began to buzz nastily, and Hook stirred.

The fairies bared their teeth and rushed at him. "Wait!" Peter yelped, leaping in front of them. "You have to heal him! I owe him."

"Heal *Hook*?" hissed the largest fairy, its tiger eyes bulging.

"I owe him a debt," Peter repeated.

"Good Lord," Hook said, faintly. He made a quiet sound of terror when Peter moved aside and let the fairies land on him. "Oh, no."

"They won't hurt you," Peter said, crouching beside Hook's head and glowering at the fairies. "Help him, or I'll tell the fairy queen that you let a friend of Peter Pan die, and she'll tear your wings off."

"Will she?" Hook murmured in a tone somewhere between amusement and horror.

The fairies hovered around the wound on his shoulder, glowing, and an evil-smelling smoke began to pour from the gap in Hook's skin. Peter looked away, the reminder of Tinker Bell landing in his gut with the strength of a punch. Hook's hand lay limp and pale on the ground beside him. Peter had the sudden urge to reach out and take it, to squeeze it in reassurance.

He stood instead, backing away and leaving the fairies to their work. He thought he saw Hook turn his head after him, but when he looked back, it appeared Hook had just fainted.

By the time the wound was closed, powdered with fairy dust and stitched shut with silver thread, Peter had foraged up a collection of berries and roots. He watched the fairies buzz curiously over the still-bandaged wound in Hook's ribs, giving it a sprinkle of dust for good measure.

"Thank you," he called.

The fairies made a sound like spitting and flew off, leaving Hook splayed beside the lake.

Peter was relieved to see that the color of his skin was normal again, his breathing even. Pixie dust had gathered in the hollow of his collar and was sprinkling slowly down his chest as the breeze disturbed it. Unobserved, Peter stared at the strong lines of Hook's shoulders, the hard slope of his chest, the black hair that wound its way down his belly and beneath his trousers. He made himself look up, but seeing Hook's face calmed by sleep was no better. He looked peaceful and handsome, his beard overgrown after all their time underground. Peter wanted to reach out and feel how it curled against his cheeks.

Hook's eyes opened. Peter leapt up, berries spilling out of his shirt. His face was hot, and he couldn't think of anything to say.

Hook stretched out a hand, snatched a wild strawberry from Peter's collection, and dropped it into his mouth.

"How do you feel?" Peter asked.

Hook hummed and pulled himself into a sitting position, reaching for another berry. Peter crouched and offered him the rest of his forage. "Remarkably less like a dead man," Hook reported, after eating a little more. "I never knew you were the sort to threaten fairies."

"Only if it's important," Peter said, finishing the berries and brushing out his shirt.

Hook frowned at him, but it did not reach into his eyes; it was almost a smile. He spent a few minutes inspecting the closed wound on his shoulder, running a finger over the stitches. "Remarkable work," he said. "Thank you."

Peter shrugged. Hook leaned over to splash cold, fresh water over himself, washing away the sweat. Peter caught himself watching a trail of water snake down Hook's chest and cleared his throat. "I owed you," he said. "Now we're even."

His own words took a moment to sink in. They were outside the cave. Peter had received the antidote, and Hook the fairy stitches. Their truce, at least in theory, was at an end. Whatever rules had allowed them to be friendly in the caves no longer applied.

He saw the realization sink into Hook's shoulders even as he was turned away, running wet hands across his cheeks. They both grew still.

Then Hook moved first, spinning around and driving Peter to the ground beneath his weight. Before Peter could react, Hook planted his forearm across his throat and bore down on it. Peter wriggled like a fish, but Hook outweighed him and no amount of flailing his legs or yanking at Hook's arm would budge him.

"So," Hook said, "the fight is back on."

Peter could not draw enough breath to say that he hadn't intended to hurt Hook. He looked up into

Hook's eyes and saw them gleaming, as they always did when he closed on a kill. But time seemed frozen; Peter saw him clearer, and closer, then he ever had before. He was caged under Hook's broad shoulders, his wide back. He tasted the heady, musky scent of Hook's body and flinched, shivered, as one of Hook's long black ringlets fell and traced across his cheek.

It was impossible to breathe, and not because of the pressure on his throat—because there was a frightening heat racing through his veins, a flush crawling through his cheeks, a sensation he didn't recognize that made him gasp for something to slake his thirst.

Hook saw it. He saw it, and paused.

His gaze traced over Peter's face, taking him in, cataloging him, and Peter could not remember ever in his life feeling so stripped bare. He didn't know what Hook ascertained, only that it made him laugh in what seemed like raw astonishment.

"Let me go," Peter stammered, his words coming out throaty and choked under the weight of Hook's arm.

There was a knowing in Hook's eyes that Peter couldn't fathom. "Far be it from me to hold a man down if he's unwilling," he said, and released Peter suddenly, climbing to his feet and leaving him on the ground.

Peter could not move, the shock of Hook's words racing through him, making his heartbeat ring in his ears. It seemed unfair that Hook had realized it an instant before he did, had given it a description.

If he's unwilling. The mocking ring in Hook's voice made it clear that he knew Peter had not been unwilling. That for a moment the weight of his body had been welcome, exciting.

Hook was backing away from him now, warmth and curiosity in his voice. "A truce, Pan," he called. "Let us call it a truce for now."

He snatched up his coat and disappeared into the trees.

~~*

Hunger eventually convinced Peter to move. The berries and nuts had been barely satisfying, and after all the fighting and his near death by the poison, his body was aching for something to sustain it. He dragged himself up and went hunting until he stumbled on a rabbit, which he roasted on a spit and devoured.

Though it had been an exceedingly pretty day when he and Hook had emerged from the cave, sun high in the sky and puffy clouds overhead, the heat intensified until it was muggy and suffocating. Soon Peter was sweating and grimy, his shirt sticking to him. He smothered the fire he had made and sat in a tree above it, nibbling at the last of the greasy meat and licking his fingers.

He was in a strange mood. The thought of Hook, which he had crammed to the back of his mind, was not staying as far back as he wanted. Even when he managed not to think about it, an uneasy awareness of the thing he was forgetting trickled along the back of his neck.

He cast around for a distraction until he remembered the very real need to find where Ernest and the other Lost Boys had gone. He made his way back to the hideout, finding it by the smell of smoke.

It was as empty as before. Peter ventured a short way into the underground, but it was nothing but soot and dirt. There was no sign of the boys.

They had to have made it out of the caves. Ernest had been with them; he would have taken care of them. Except Ernest was wounded, Peter remembered with a twinge of concern. Where could they have gone? Where would they have hidden?

The rain started as he emerged from the hideout. It was a thick, clogging rain that turned the earth to muck and made Peter feel as if he were drowning standing up. He flew above the forest, circling out in a spiral from the hideout and finding nothing but beasts. When he was soaked through, he retreated to shelter under a tree, where a cluster of fairies spun a web above him to keep out the rain. He sat there in damp misery, alone with his thoughts. He tried to think about the Lost Boys, about Ernest, but his mind kept circling back to Hook.

It had been so instant and obvious, the full-body yearning he had felt when Hook's weight crashed down on him. The way it had shifted from the threat of violence to the threat of pleasure.

What did it mean? Peter ran his hands down his legs, shivering absently at the memory of his skin prickling, pulse pounding. He had never felt that way before about anyone or anything. But it had been happening all along with Hook, he realized, from the very first moment they had reunited in Neverland.

You liked it when Hook was trying to hurt you, Ernest had said.

That wasn't quite right, because he had liked it when Hook wasn't trying to hurt him too. It wasn't the threat that had captured Peter's attention. It was the way Hook had leapt in to meet him when he started telling stories of war and violence, as eager as Peter was to fight and scheme. It was the way he had given Peter his full attention, the full force of his ruthlessness, without ever worrying if Peter could handle it.

That was it. Everyone else had followed him at best, at worst tried to stop him or change him. Hook had matched him, and had never tried to protect Peter, had always done his worst. That was what felt so good.

Peter pressed his palms into his eyes. That had to be wrong, he thought. It *sounded* wrong. But it was far too powerful a feeling to ignore.

And when he had been really hurting, when he had been mourning Tink, Hook had softened so suddenly he had been like another man entirely—he had relinquished the game at once, grieved with Peter, been kind to him. Peter hugged his knees, trying to decide what it all meant.

Eventually he slept, and woke to dew beading on the ends of his hair and dripping down his cheeks. The fairies had left him in a circle of pixie dust, and although Peter could see the tracks of snakes and other wild beasts outside it, nothing had crossed the circle.

The sky was still gray and sweaty, an uncertain fog hanging over the forest. Peter drew breath, deciding to follow his nose into whatever adventure first presented itself. Maybe if he spent the rest of his life dreaming, like Hook, eventually he'd forget it was a dream and be content again. Maybe it wouldn't matter why something felt good as long as it did.

But before he could choose a path, a fairy sprang

down from the tree above him on a silk cord, glittering and flaking dust. In one of its many limbs was curled a slip of paper. "A message," the fairy chimed in a tone which made it clear that it did not appreciate being made a messenger. Peter thanked it and unrolled the paper.

The hand was instantly familiar, flowing over the paper in a ponderous and elegant script. It read:

My dear Peter Pan,

You are hereby invited to dinner aboard the Jolly Roger to discuss the conditions of a ceasefire between yours truly and the Lost Boys. At this dinner, both parties shall agree to do each other no harm. Should you accept, the Jolly Roger will be anchored in Jewelbox Bay until tomorrow, and dinner shall be held at six p.m. sharp.

Yours sincerely,
Jas. Hook.

Peter crumpled the note. He shouldn't go. There was no reason for him to go. Hook wouldn't attack the Lost Boys anyway if Peter left them alone.

Seeing Hook would be dangerous.

He *shouldn't* go.

Sunlight darted through the clouds above as he tore up the note and scattered it. He caught the fairy who had delivered the note by one of its long limbs and held it up as it wriggled and cursed at him.

"Take a message to Hook," he said. "Tell him I'll be there."

Thirteen

Jewelbox Bay was near the shallows outside Death's Head Cavern, but it couldn't have been a more different location. It was a pretty sapphire bay ringed with hills, above which there were flowering orchards that gave fruit in three seasons. Peter could distinctly recall a time when he and the Lost Boys had let fly a deadly hail of arrows from those trees and given the *Jolly Roger* and its crew the appearance of pincushions below.

A proper meeting between captains, Peter knew, should begin precisely on time, with all parties dressed in their finest and accompanied by a grand entourage. Accordingly, he descended onto the deck of the *Jolly Roger* fifteen minutes late and all alone.

He expected some kind of bristling hostility from the remains of Hook's crew—they could at least have clutched their weapons and menaced him as he walked between them. But the pirates were all in poor shape and shrank from him. Peter felt a little guilty for scaring them.

He knocked at the captain's cabin. From within, Hook called, "Come in."

Peter went inside, his stomach growling before he could even take in the dinner that had been laid in the center of the cabin. It was a feast: an enormous stuffed fish in the center was surrounded by dishes of wild roasted chicken, platters of greased and steaming vegetables, butter and bread. Peter swallowed, willing himself not to be distracted, and looked to the captain himself.

That was even more distracting. Hook sat like a china teacup in its saucer, dressed for dinner in a sea-green silk waistcoat. His curls were gleaming, pulled back into a knot at the base of his neck. His beard looked freshly trimmed, and even his nails looked neat beneath the lacy cuff of his shirt. His hook rested in his lap, out of sight.

Peter was conscious of his dirty clothes. He hadn't been able to do much to improve them aside from washing in the stream, and the bloodstains had been too stubborn to remove. But Hook didn't seem to notice any of that; he was gazing at Poseidon's circlet where it rested on Peter's head, startled into wondering silence.

"Hello, Captain," Peter said, and gave a cautious bow. The crown threatened to fall off his head if he leaned too far in any direction.

Hook cleared his throat, some color in his face, and gestured to the remaining seat. "Please, sit."

Peter took a step forward, but stopped behind the chair. "I'm not here for the Lost Boys," he said. "I don't even know where they are."

"Oh well." Hook did not look sorry, or even surprised. "No sense in wasting a good meal. Sit."

Peter sat. This close, the fragrance of the food made his mouth water. Hook leaned across the table and picked up a jug of wine. "Something to drink?" he asked.

"How do I know it isn't poisoned?"

"You have my word as a gentleman," Hook said. "I did say no harm would come to you at this meeting."

"As if I'd trust you." But he took the jug from Hook's hand and poured himself a cup, wine sloshing over the sides and staining his fingertips.

He wondered if Hook would mention their last encounter. This seemed a world away from Hook shirtless and wounded, pinning him down in the grass. Instead of saying anything, he smiled at Peter, his eyes darting from Peter's face to the crown as if the sight of it gave him pleasure.

Peter looked away, his skin prickling. He filled his plate with all the meat and bread within reach and began chewing on chunks of each.

"Are you and the Lost Boys to continue fighting together?" Hook asked idly. He ate too, albeit more slowly, with a knife and fork.

"I don't know," Peter said. "You'll have to ask them." He swallowed a hunk of bread with a gulp of wine. It was sweet and dark, fruity and soft on his tongue.

"Do you like the wine?" Hook asked. "I stole it from Blackbeard years ago. He said it was worth fighting a war over. I've been saving it for a special occasion."

Peter took another swig to avoid answering him. It went straight to his cheeks; he felt them heating as he set down his goblet.

Worth fighting a war over, he thought.

"To our fallen companions." Hook offered his glass to Peter for a toast. "May we see more of them in their next lives."

Peter took a deep breath and raised his glass. "To Tink." It still stung to say her name. It was strange to think she had been here, in Hook's cabin, apparently enjoying his company just the way—

Just the way Peter did.

Hook hummed his approval. "To Tinker Bell. A dear friend, and as fine a woman as ever resembled an insect."

They drank.

"If you're not here for the Lost Boys," Hook said, "then you must be here for me."

Peter sucked in a breath. He couldn't speak, because to say anything would be to admit the truth: that he had always been there for Hook, he simply hadn't known it. The thought filled him with butterflies, with tingling nerves that weren't all unpleasant but still made him want to bolt away.

He cast around the cabin instead, taking in its extravagance, studying the tapestries on the walls and pretending to be absorbed.

Hook went on talking cordially. Peter ignored him, and only looked back when Hook said, "Don't you agree?"

"What?"

"That it wasn't really the Lost Boys and the pirates who needed to make peace anyway." Hook set down his knife and fork and wiped a smidgen of grease from his lip. He leaned back in his chair and picked up his goblet of wine, surveying Peter as he might survey a treasure map. "It was always you and I. Those boys, my crew—they don't really care what becomes of the island or the sea or any other battleground. It's *our* war."

"That's right," Peter said.

"Do we need them anymore?" Hook asked. "Do we need these unwilling soldiers to fight our battles? Or should we keep it between us?"

Peter looked at him across the table. "What do you mean?" This was it, he thought. Ready or not, this was what he had come here for.

"I mean," Hook began, "that perhaps we should consider a different spin on our engagements."

He leaned forward. That was when the blow fell.

As a matter of fact, it came from below. The impact struck the *Jolly Roger* in the keel with such force as to lift them both from their seats and send them flying across the cabin.

Peter crashed into the door, stunned. The door burst open beneath his weight and sent him tumbling out onto the deck amidst Hook's frantic crew. All of them went sliding down the deck as the boat tipped stern-up and listed dangerously to one side, timbers squealing in protest.

Peter bounced and slid into the port-side railing and clung to it. With an ominous groan, the *Jolly Roger*'s prow dipped lower still, plunging into the sapphire bay. A pair of enormous tentacles slid from the water, wrapped around the figurehead, and snapped it off.

A moment later, the kraken dragged its head over the prow. It stretched open its enormous mouth and shrieked, so high and piercing that Peter instinctively pressed his ear into his shoulder, tears springing into his eyes. The kraken's tentacles unwound across the deck, snarling around the masts for grip, its suckers tearing holes in the railings and ripping cannons and men from the ship. The *Jolly Roger* gave a shudder and a crunch as the kraken's full weight unfurled across her prow. The beast dropped a screaming pirate into its mouth, and a dripping tentacle covered in seaweed and suckers reached for Peter.

Peter got his feet up against the railing and pushed off. He made it into the air only to get caught in the sail of a falling mast and crash bruisingly to the deck, tangled in ropes and heavy cloth. Panting, he struggled over on his stomach and crawled for what he fervently hoped was the edge of the sail. The deck was tipping and squealing as it cracked apart. Peter stuck his head out from under the sail, but couldn't free himself quickly enough to avoid the tentacle that rolled over him, snarling around his stomach and lifting him toward the kraken's mouth.

Pounding at the tentacle with his fists did nothing. Its scaly skin was too thick to feel the blows. Peter yelled and kicked, fear making him dizzy, his vision blurring as the coil around his stomach tightened. The kraken brought him to dangle above its maw. Its blank square pupils fixed on him, and Peter stared back at it, wheezing, petrified.

Then a shot rang out and one of the great eyes spouted blood. The kraken gave an unearthly scream and thrashed in agony, hurling Peter into the air. He tumbled into a low cloud before he could right himself, coughing and gasping for breath.

Below, the kraken's weight was splitting the *Jolly Roger* in half. Peter heard two more shots fired, but not could not see who was shooting—until he saw the kraken reaching toward the captain's cabin.

He saw Hook dragged out by the feet, dangling from the kraken's grip like a toy.

Peter didn't think. He dove. As he plunged through the air, he saw Hook struggling to point his pistol at the kraken's enormous mouth, unable to get off the final shot.

Knowing he couldn't pull Hook out of its clutches, Peter went for the kraken's remaining eye. He seized a jagged, splintered stave that had once been part of the rigging and tore it free of a tangling rope, and then flew toward the kraken, past its captive. He drove the makeshift spear deep into its pupil and then leapt back, only to be nearly deafened by its screams.

Peter twisted around midair to see Hook dropping toward the creature's mouth. He moved faster than he thought possible. One moment he was poised above the eye, and the next he was seizing fistfuls of Hook's waistcoat and straining upward to stop his fall, spiraling past the collapsing mast as Hook threw his arms around him. Peter made straight for the trees in the hills above the bay, wishing he could close his ears to the kraken's horrible noises and the crunching, cracking, squealing of the *Jolly Roger* being torn apart.

~~*

He let them both down in the woods when he could no longer fly, and crumpled to the ground. He wanted to go further; he could still hear the screams echoing off the hills in the distance, and panic still washed over him in waves. But his limbs were trembling and it was all he could do to stay on all fours while his pulse banged around in his throat.

Hook lay on his back beside him, breathing hard. When Peter collected himself enough to glance over, Hook met his eyes and began to laugh, a little hysterically. When he ran out of breath he lay there silently instead, a hand on his heart.

"You lost your crown," he said. "I suppose Poseidon wanted it back."

Peter couldn't remember seeing his crown in the chaos; he supposed it had probably gone flying off when the first blow had hit the *Jolly Roger*. "I'm still a king," he said, with a weak attempt at humor.

"Pan," Hook said. "You saved my life."

Peter didn't know what to say. He had gone back to rescue Hook so unthinkingly, so instinctually, that he was only now beginning to realize he had done it. He hadn't worried about a single thing besides protecting Hook.

He cast around for a reason—an excuse, not the real reason, which he already knew.

"I had to," he said finally. "If you'd died there, I wouldn't have been the one to defeat you."

Hook gave a low chuckle. "Your obsession is flattering, Pan. And I share it."

"Obsession?"

"Is that not what they call it," Hook said, "when two men can think of nothing but each other?"

Peter went still, feeling his ears go hot at the implication. Hook knew, he thought. Hook knew exactly what Peter had felt before, when Hook had pinned him down.

He sat there tongue-tied. The two of them didn't speak for some time, until the kraken's last cringing wails had receded and there was no sound but the shiver of the leaves.

"Thank you," Hook said eventually. "I suppose I should have led with that."

Peter sat up, leaves scattering around him. "You shot the kraken first to save me. You don't owe me."

Hook tutted. "How modest. A man knows when he owes something." He sat up and turned toward Peter. "Perhaps this will even the score."

Peter lifted his head. Hook's hair was tangled around his face like a lion's mane and his eyes were painfully clear, all teasing and mirth gone from his mouth.

He took Peter's chin in his hand, his fingers calloused but gentle, and kissed him.

Everything in the world grew quiet and Peter's body grew loud. The caress of Hook's fingertips under his chin made his pulse catch, his throat flushing, shoulders tightening. He could only seem to breathe in, breathe Hook in deeper. Hook's lips were dry, and he tasted like salt and sweet wine. He smelled like gunpowder and the sea and he was everywhere, shifting closer across the leaves, his other arm snaking around Peter's waist, the iron claw pressed flat between his shoulder blades.

Peter dug his fingers into fistfuls of earth, trying to ground himself as Hook pulled them together, tipping Peter's head back with the gentle thrust of his kiss, a momentum that threatened to tilt them both to the ground. Peter was impossibly hot, hot to his fingertips and toes and his skin was crawling with the need to be touched, the shock of that need.

Sweat caught at the back of his shirt. His skin was stark canvas begging for ink, and Hook's touch was going to stain him forever. It was too much, too sudden. Peter recoiled, yanking a knife from his boot and holding it between them. He didn't mean it as a threat, just a way to make distance where none had been.

Hook stared at him, bemused, his mouth slightly pink.

"What's the matter?" he asked. "Have I misunderstood you?"

"No," Peter said faintly. "But I—I've never—"

Hook stroked his face, brushed his fingertips across Peter's jaw. Peter took a breath that shuddered behind his teeth. Hook looked at him like he was some kind of jewel, like he was something precious.

"Proud and insolent youth," he said.

Peter shivered at the affection in his voice. His grip was slippery on the hilt of his knife; he realized he was afraid, more afraid than he had ever been in his life, but it was the kind of eager fright that came with anticipation and hunger. And Hook could certainly see it in him. His bright-blue eyes were taking Peter in, and Peter couldn't look away.

He bit his lip, struggling to make words out of the war waging itself in his chest.

"I don't know what this makes me," he managed at last.

Hook laughed, not unkindly. "It makes you whatever you want it to make you." He pushed a curl of Peter's hair behind his ear, and sparks seemed to jump across Peter's skin in the wake of his fingers. "You once told me you were youth and joy."

Peter smiled a little, though he felt brittle and uncertain. "I made that up because you hated being called old."

"Ah, of course. Then what are you, Pan? A spirit? A prince? Or merely a man frightened of indulging himself?"

Peter felt the truth on his tongue, but he couldn't say it, couldn't even really think it. He felt empty, and yet more fully attached to his body than he had ever been, more aware of his senses and where he and Hook touched.

"Hook—" he began.

"Peter," Hook said. "Kiss me."

Peter swallowed. He brought the tip of his knife to rest against Hook's chest, digging it in as if testing the earth.

Hook's eyes gleamed with something almost playful. He curled his fingers around the back of Peter's neck. "Or we can keep trying to kill each other, if you prefer."

He leaned forward suddenly, as if to skewer himself on Peter's blade, and Peter—before he knew what he was doing—wrenched the knife back. He saw Hook's smile in the moment before Hook was too close to see, his mouth catching Peter's again, his arms around him.

Peter took a fistful of Hook's waistcoat to steady himself, squeezing his eyes shut and panting at the brush of Hook's tongue on his lips. Hook did not seem to care that Peter still held a knife; he pressed his palm to Peter's stomach where heat was already pooling, his fingers stroking, coaxing. Peter's pulse was loud in his ears, his heart racing so violently that he didn't know how it would last without bursting in his chest.

Hook sent him sprawling into the moss with a gentle push. He cradled Peter's face in his hands and kissed him deeply, licking into his mouth. Peter let go of his knife impulsively to grab a fistful of Hook's hair, pulling out the ribbon that kept his curls contained at the nape of his neck. Ringlets cascaded over his fingers.

Hook sank over him, brought his mouth to Peter's neck, and bit him.

Hard. Stinging. Something in Peter shifted and he seized hold of Hook with both hands, yanking the buttons on his waistcoat open and pulling it down his arms. Hook kissed him madly, and Peter imagined his eyes blazing red as they had in Peter's dreams for years. Peter inhaled the smell of him, the sweat and wine and smoke, the spice and wax sweetness of summer sunlight, all heightened as Hook wrestled out of his shirtsleeves and Peter dragged him close again. Peter pressed a hand to his chest, found it tangled with soft hair, felt the thoughts squeeze out of his head as Hook caught his lip between his teeth and bit hard enough to burn. He bit back, and Hook gasped against his mouth.

"Take what you want," Hook said, breathless. "That's what you've always done. Take me."

"Do that again," Peter said. He clenched his eyes shut when Hook, instead of obeying directly, dragged his tongue over the place he had bitten. There was a prickling pain that sent tingles and shivers through him, and it left him speechless. Hook's teeth dug into his lip again and his whole body tensed with it, a moan catching in the back of his throat. It was almost too much just to feel it, like lying in the surf and feeling the waves crawl over him.

He lay gasping as Hook reached inside his trousers and ran rough, calloused fingers over the tenderest part of him. Fire spread to every inch of him, sharp as a needle, and he thought he would burst or shatter. It felt unspeakably good, and unbearable, and he cried out raw and pleading. Hook held him to the ground, palm pressed to Peter's chest where Peter's heart was thundering. Peter clawed at his back, seized fistfuls of his hair, gasping for breaths that never seemed enough.

The peak of sensation reached a point like a knife—hot—devastating—and then broke suddenly, plunging him back into his own skin to feel his muscles shaking, to hear himself whimper when Hook kissed him.

"Peter," Hook whispered.

Peter couldn't speak. He had never felt more filthy. Never inhabited his own skin so fully. Nothing, in all the time he had spent in the grime of the forest or the blood and sweat of the hunt, had ever managed to reach him as deeply as this: pressed to Hook's bare chest, able to feel his heavy breathing, the unresolved arousal still drawing him taut.

Peter wanted to reach out and touch him, but he was afraid of how much more intense that would feel. He could imagine staring into Hook's eyes as he was overcome with sensation, knowing that it was his hands doing the work, and a shiver of longing ran down his spine.

"Peter," Hook said again. "Are you all right?"

Peter opened his eyes and plunged back into a reality he hadn't realized he'd left behind. The forest was all around them, but it seemed gray and distant, except for Hook. He was struck by the feeling that they were the only two people alive in the world—that this was something beyond any magic or illusion or story Neverland could conjure. Something real.

It made Peter suddenly, painfully conscious of what wasn't real. He swallowed, trying to ignore the sensation of being unmoored, floating in a body that wasn't his own. This was perfect, if he could hold onto it.

Hook stroked tenderly at his temple, pushing damp curls of his hair out of his face. "Peter?"

Everything around them was so quiet, like the forest was holding its breath, holding a space for all their secrets.

"I don't know," Peter said. He didn't think he'd ever wanted anything more than to stay like this. He took a deep, steadying breath, and Hook pressed a kiss to his forehead. Peter wasn't surprised anymore at how gentle he could be. "Is it always like this?" he asked.

"What do you mean?"

"You've done this before." He hated the vulnerability in his voice. It gave away that he had no idea what he was meant to be feeling, no idea how people managed to be this close to each other without falling apart. "Do you always feel—scared?"

"Oh," Hook said. "Yes." And he was enfolding Peter in his arms again. "Can't you hear my heart beating? I thought it must be making a racket."

Peter brushed his fingers over the pulse in Hook's throat; it was pounding as hard as his own. He gave a weak laugh. Now that he was paying attention, he could feel the tension in Hook's body where it met his, an anxious, erotic tension.

With a guilty twist, he realized he'd let Hook focus on him completely, and he had been so caught up in what he was feeling that he had barely reciprocated. If nothing else, he knew it was supposed to be mutual. Trying to swallow his uncertainty, he ran his fingers down Hook's chest and over his abdomen, reaching—

Hook caught his hand. "You don't need to," he said. He gently pulled Peter's wrist aside.

"But... it's not fair."

"Why not?"

"Because I didn't—you didn't—"

"I'm perfectly satisfied," Hook said. "All I've wanted since the moment you came back was to have my hands on you. Truly."

Peter licked his lips. "What if I *want* to touch you?"

"Ah..." Hook looked as if that were something he hadn't considered, as if it hadn't occurred to him that

Peter wanted him as much as he wanted Peter. He shivered, and then released his hand, touching his cheek instead. "Well, I won't say no to that."

Peter leaned in. He cupped Hook's face, his palms prickled by his beard, and slowly kissed him. It was different when he took the lead. He could feel how Hook responded to his touch, the tremble under his skin. It was strange and gratifying to realize that Hook felt as he did.

"Peter," Hook murmured, when he pulled away. His eyes were soft.

Somewhere along the line, he had started using Peter's name. Peter couldn't remember when, but it was perfect; it made him feel settled, fully himself. All of a sudden it didn't seem right to call Hook *Hook*, distant and fantastical, not when they were together like this.

Peter knew his other name, his intimate and human name, the one he signed his letters with, the one that always rolled off his tongue carelessly when he was introducing himself. He bent and kissed it shyly into Hook's throat: "James."

Hook stiffened. "What did you say?"

Something about his tone made Peter draw back. It was not the reaction he'd expected. Hook was gazing at him with startled pain, like he'd been stung. "James?" He saw the name land on Hook this time, saw him flinch, saw it travel through his body like ripples on a pond. "That's... right, isn't it?" Peter asked, suddenly afraid it was as painful a memory as Peter's old name.

"Yes," Hook said. "That's right."

His eyes were far away and shuttered. He sat up, and Peter followed him nervously, laying a hand on his knee. "What's wrong?"

"I've just remembered something I forgot," Hook said heavily.

"What?"

"Samuel." He said the name like it was shrapnel he was pulling from a wound. "*Samuel.*"

Fourteen

Peter's throat was dry. "What does he have to do with this?" It was a cold thing to say, he knew that, but he was confused by the distance in James's eyes.

"I forgot him," James said, as if he couldn't wrap his mind around the words.

"You didn't forget him. We've talked about him—"

"Not *him*. Not that puppet." There was something like disgust in James's voice. "The real Samuel. We met… we met at university. It was before all this—it was so long ago."

"He was real?"

"Yes. I loved him. I'd only ever dreamed of men before, but he was real. I knew I'd never have to come back here so long as I was with him."

A shiver ran down Peter's back, a twist of hurt and dismay. "Where is he, then?"

"They sent him away to the war," James said hoarsely. "He never came back. That's what I used to dream about. Endless dreams of losing him, of seeing it happen, of reading the letter. I couldn't sleep. I couldn't live. So I…"

Peter could guess where he was going, and didn't want to hear it. The world was still gray around them; there was only him, James, and the grief pulling James away.

"James," he said, pleading. "Forget about it."

He squeezed at James's knee, but James jerked

away from him with a snarl of pain. "No," he said. "I *did* forget. I forgot everything. I went looking for him in the only place I thought I might find him—and yes, here he was, as if he'd never gone, just another sailor in my crew. And I wanted him to be real so badly that I—forgot—everything." The fog had gone from his eyes; they were clear and sharp and he was crying, bright sudden tears. "Oh my God, *everything*. How long have I been here?" he demanded of the empty air, bowing his head. "What in God's name happened to my *life*?"

"You said yourself," Peter said. He couldn't move, fighting panic. It was all he could do not to think of the Darling house. "Neverland is better than all that."

James snapped toward him with a kind of desperation. "Peter," he said. "Think, please. You ran away from your family, but Neverland's used that against you, don't you see? It's used that to trap you here. You *must* remember, or it'll never let you go."

"I *do* remember," Peter cried. The memory was vivid and all around him; it was only getting worse the more James talked. He had managed to forget there was anything beyond Neverland, and now it was rushing back over him. "I do remember, and I don't want it. I just want to stay here with you and forget about it."

"I will not forget again," James said. "I will not." He repeated it like a mantra, like a prayer. "I will not. I only remembered now because I haven't felt anything real in God knows how many years. I'd forgotten what it was like to be seen. Spoken to. Touched. We've been locked in here with ghosts."

"Shut up," Peter said, half furious and half pleading. "You're *ruining* it."

James finally seemed to realize that Peter was angry with him; he stared at him, tears making slow tracks down his face. "Peter," he said. "I've been here alone with nothing. You're the only good thing, the only real thing, that's come along in all that time. You're the only one who's called me by my name." He squeezed his shaking fingers around Peter's hand. "We have to get out of here. Now. Before it makes us forget again."

"*No!*" Peter tore away from him, scrambling to his feet, backing away like James might infect him. "*I* don't care if it's not real," he said. "It's real enough for me. It's better. It's all I have. I want to—I want to stay here till I die."

James looked stunned. "What are you talking about? What kind of a life can you possibly think you'd have here?"

"I'll be Peter Pan. Forever." It would be enough. It would have to be. He could forget about this too. "I'll be like the fairies."

"That's nonsense and you know it," James said, getting shakily to his feet. "Come with me. Please." He stretched out his arm.

"Go if you want," Peter said in the coldest voice he could muster. "I'm staying."

He flew before James could stop him.

Fifteen

The rain started the moment Peter was gone.

It began as a sad dripping that quickly escalated to a miserable deluge, fat raindrops pummeling the trees and earth, turning the ground to mud. Thunder soon joined the chorus, lightning flickering on the horizon. All the while, the air grew colder, and a thick fog choked the forest.

"This seems excessive," James muttered, teeth gritted as he shouldered his way through the undergrowth. Then again, nothing was too excessive for Neverland.

In the smoggy rain, it was impossible to make out any landmarks; even the mountains were hidden from view. As such, it took him the better part of a day to locate the Lost Boys' charred hideout. It was James's best guess as to where he would find Peter—or at least Ernest, who Peter was unlikely to abandon if he meant to stay in Neverland forever.

But not only was the hideout lacking any signs of Peter, the Lost Boys were nowhere to be found either. Surely, James thought, that meant the boys had been led somewhere safer; they lacked the initiative to make such choices without Peter. He held on to that hope.

Nearby, he found a set of fairies burrowing into a tree. "Excuse me," James said. It annoyed him to even have to talk to them, because it felt like playing by

Neverland's rules, but he had to accept that for a little longer. "Have you seen the Lost Boys?"

The fairies said a series of rude words, some of which were beyond James's understanding of their language. He got the impression they weren't willing to assist an enemy of Peter Pan.

"I'm trying to help him," James said. He came closer to the tree, and a fairy darted out and stung him on the cheek. "*Ow*, damn you!" Without thinking, he grabbed the fairy by the wings, dangling it in the air. "Tell me where Pan is," he growled, "or I'll say the magic words. There's no such thing as fai..."

The fairy explained hastily that it hadn't seen head or tail of Peter Pan, but that the Lost Boys had gone down the river after salvaging weapons from the remains of the hideout. James released it with a snarl, and then realized what he had done. "Excuse me," he said abruptly, mortified with himself. "Er—sorry. Old habits. Very sorry." He backed away before they could consider adding another sting to match the one on his face, and hurried off down the river.

For a moment, with the fairy hanging helplessly from his grip, he had thought of himself as Hook.

~~*

The river emptied into Mermaid Lagoon, pouring over a cliff into the roiling water below. The weather was only growing worse, clouds twisting yellow and black over the horizon. James nearly fell to his death while trying to find a way down the slick cliffs in the driving rain. He didn't know whether it would particularly hurt him to die in Neverland—it wasn't real, he kept reminding himself—but he was afraid he would at least wake to find himself outside Neverland, with no way to find Peter.

He was drenched by the time he reached the shore, his palms scraped bloody on the rocks.

Meanwhile, the merfolk looked to be having a merry time, riding the waves around the lagoon and jeering at James. He had always disliked them— ghostly, glossy creatures with thready hair and staring fish eyes. He liked them no better now that he thought of them as illusions.

"Have you seen the Lost Boys?" he bellowed at a passing mermaid, who swam closer, chirping and holding her hands over her frilled ears. "I need to find Pan," he shouted, trying to make himself heard over the howling wind.

The mermaid flipped her tail, splashing James with enough water to soak him through a second time. Then she gave a nasty squawking noise that might've been laughter and swam away, her teeth bared.

James retreated under the nearest cliff, not that it was much comfort to be out of the rain when he was already wet. At least his hands were numb enough to have stopped feeling their injuries. James caught himself thinking unfriendly thoughts toward the mermaids, as if they were really his enemies, as if any of it were real.

"It's a lie," he said loudly. "My name is James. I'm not a pirate. I'm going home, and I'm taking Pan— *Peter*, damn it—with me. And you can't stop me by flooding the place, so you may as well give up."

As if in reply, a streak of lightning cut the sky open. James flinched back against the cliff. The merfolk screamed in excitement or fear and went slicing through the water into a flooded cave across the bay.

The following peal of thunder made the cliff shake to an alarming degree; James held his breath, wondering if Neverland had plans to bury him rather than let him go. But the thunder passed, and the merfolk came streaking out of their cave again, throwing themselves into the waves.

James squinted. There was fire flickering on the cave wall.

Lifting a hand to shield his face, he struggled back out into the rain.

A narrow, rocky spit of land was all that connected the cave entrance to the shore, and the waves were high enough to roll over it with every gust of wind. James grimaced. "It's not real," he told himself. "Nothing in this wretched dream has managed to kill me yet."

Out loud, it didn't sound as reassuring as it had in his head. It sounded dangerously like a dare.

He made his way out onto the spit, pressing his back against the cliff behind him and finding it difficult to keep his footing over the slick rock. Worse, when he was halfway across, the merfolk took notice of him. They swam over and began tugging at his trousers, first playfully and then quite hard, trying to pull him in. The first few retreated when James kicked at their slimy hands, but they weren't deterred for more than a few moments—and more of them gathered as he inched along, their gleaming eyes following him.

"Protecting something in that cave, are you?" James shouted. He glanced at the entrance, which was still at least twenty meters off. "It looks as if there's a fire inside! Now who might that be?"

The merfolk hissed, growing agitated. One of them slithered forward and wrapped its hands around his ankle and jerked hard, and James fell on his back in the rocks with a grunt. He kicked out hard and felt his foot collide with something soft—like a mermaid's face, perhaps. There was a screech of pain, and he caught sight of green blood running down a scaly cheek before it vanished under the water. James drew his sword and slashed at the waves, hoping to frighten off the rest of the merfolk.

Instead, he realized his mistake as their taunting eyes turned angry and, as one, they snarled and leapt for him. He tried to run for it, but only made it a few strides toward the cave. One sprang almost out of the water, slamming him against the cliff and then digging teeth and fingernails into his clothes as it dragged him into the waves.

There was nothing he could do. He lost his sword almost at once, and the freezing water closed over his head, a brutal, numbing cold spreading through his body. He could see nothing in the frothing water, only feel a dozen talons clawing at him as they pulled him down.

Then, from a great distance, he heard someone shouting. The merfolk released him suddenly, and a new set of hands closed on his shirt, pulling him back to the surface. He took in such a great gasping breath as to make his head spin, so it was a long moment before he recovered enough to look at his rescuer. He saw brown hair and for an aching moment thought it was Peter.

Then he blinked, and it was Ernest.

The boy was sodden, his eyes owlish in the grim wet darkness of the world. He dragged James the remaining distance to the cave, limping and heavily favoring his left leg. James recalled stabbing him, and wondered if he should apologize. Just because Ernest was fictional didn't mean he couldn't appreciate an apology.

At the back of the cave, the only part of it that wasn't swamped with water, the Lost Boys were huddled around a bonfire. They scrambled to their feet at the sight of James, most of them visibly terrified. Ernest dropped James on the floor and drew a knife from his belt, trembling as he held it out.

"What on earth—" James coughed and spat out seawater. "What on earth did you rescue me for if you were only going to threaten me?"

"Where's Peter?" Ernest demanded.

James stared at him in the firelight, hope draining out of him. "You mean you don't know either."

Ernest's knife arm drooped. "Don't you?" His face hardened—or at least he made an attempt at it. "You're probably lying."

"If I knew where he was, I'd be there," James snapped. "I certainly wouldn't be looking for you."

"If he doesn't know anything," Curly said hesitantly, "should we kill him?"

"*No*," Ernest said, rounding on him. "We don't kill *anyone*. Not even Hook."

James inched closer to the fire, since the Lost Boys weren't exactly keeping him from it. Ernest watched him, but let him sit in the warmth. He remained standing, gripping his knife.

"You don't have to worry about me," James said. "I've gone off piracy. Cross my heart and hope to die."

"Do you expect me to believe that?" Ernest asked, his mouth thinning.

"Yes. You've always struck me as rather gullible."

"Well, I don't. You can stay and dry off, but after

that, you'll have to leave."

James had to laugh. "I can't tell if you're really this gregarious or if you're being generous because Neverland doesn't want me to die. Or perhaps it's because you're Pan's imaginary friend and *he* doesn't want me to die."

That was a nice thought. He could cling to that.

Ernest, predictably, looked confused. "What?"

"Did you know you're not real?" It felt cruel to say, but on the other hand, James felt he needed to keep saying things out loud to remind himself of what was true. "Did you know that Pan made you all up so he'd have playmates? Funny, isn't it? You and my pirates are the same. He and I just wanted different things."

"What's he talking about?" one of the Lost Boys asked plaintively.

Ernest looked like James had slapped him for no reason. After a second, he said, abruptly, "He didn't make me up."

"As you like," James said.

"No." Although Ernest was still gazing in James's direction, he didn't seem to be seeing him. "He didn't. The Lost Boys were his... but I adopted them. I wanted friends who'd like me, who'd look up to me, and when I came here and saw them wandering without a leader..."

"Oh," James said. "*Oh*. You too?"

~~*

They sat together by the fire for a long while. The Lost Boys wandered off to other corners of the cave, seeming not to enjoy the topic of their conversation. James couldn't really blame them for that. It had to be distasteful to hear yourself discussed as an imaginary construct. He didn't know if they really understood, or if they could.

"I ought to have realized," Ernest said. "About Peter, I mean. I remember us talking about where he came from. He ran away like I did."

"He told you about his life?" James asked, startled.

"Only a little. It was just after he arrived, when we were going up the mountain. He said he didn't have a family."

It would have hurt less if someone had stamped on his heart. "No," James said. "No, I don't think he does."

"I wanted him to be with me," Ernest said. "Er— with us." When James glanced at him, he turned pink. "I guess I knew he was different than the others. And I liked him so much, despite everything."

"You should go home, dear boy, wherever home is for you." James cleared his throat. "Also, Peter is a menace. I wouldn't wish being in love with him on anyone."

Ernest suddenly became very interested in staring at his toes and said nothing.

"I'm sorry about your leg," James added. "I hope it won't hinder you along the way."

"I'll make it," Ernest said. "I don't really feel it anymore."

Outside, the storm raged on. Ernest offered to let James stay until he was dry, but James had little hope that the rain would stop, so once he'd regained feeling in his extremities he set off. Ernest had given him an idea of one more place where Peter might be found.

~~*

By that point, he was relatively sure that Neverland wasn't going to kill him. It would, however, do its absolute best to make him miserable. His long trudge through the soggy forest had been proof enough of that; the merfolk attempting to drown him had been further insult to injury.

Neither, as it turned out, was anything compared to the mountain.

By the time he reached the foothills, it had grown so cold that there was frost gathering on the leaves. Icy wind whipped over the mountainside, while the frost made the cliffs all the more treacherous. As if that weren't enough, it began to hail, thick chunks of ice that stung and scraped his cheeks as they rained down.

James made incremental progress, his fingers and toes so cold they seemed about to fall off. He felt absurd, almost biblical, as he dragged himself up another slick, freezing slope; this was like a trial arranged by a vengeful god. Exhaustion made him delirious, but he didn't stop to rest for fear that if he fell asleep, he would forget himself again. Even without sleep, he found himself drifting to peaceful dreams of sailing on the summer sea.

"It never happened," James croaked, unable to hear himself over the howling wind. "It wasn't real. Home was real. Peter is real."

If only he'd been able to remember more of home. He couldn't even think of his address, nor the names of his late parents, nor if he'd ever had any siblings— he didn't think so, but couldn't be certain. He could barely picture the place where he lived: his cottage, which had surely been empty for years, and the river which ran alongside it.

When at last he reached the forest where he had fought Peter and been driven off by the fairy queen, he was so weary he was pulling himself along on branches and tree trunks. He didn't know what he expected to find when he reached the commune tree—he had never seen it, only watched Peter go through his telescope—but it wasn't an empty field of dead flowers wilted by the frost.

Peter wasn't there.

James sagged against a tree and slid down to rest in the frozen leaves below, fuming with despair. He let his head fall back against the trunk with a painful thud. "I thought for sure he'd be here," he said aloud. "It seemed so dramatic, just like him. Why on earth did getting here have to be such an ordeal if it didn't *mean* anything?"

"A fascinating question," the fairy queen said.

James leapt. The queen was sitting on a branch above him. All around her, the frost had melted, and green leaves were growing.

She fixed him with her nasty, beady red eyes. "I see you've come to your senses," she said. "I never expected it, after all these years. Will you be leaving us at last?"

"I ought to swat you," James said, stiffly straightening up against the tree. "You *wretched* little insect. How long have I been here?"

"Many years," she said. "It might have been eternity if not for him."

James's chest squeezed, although that could have been his heart giving out from the exertion. "Yes, thanks to him. No thanks to you. Where is he? I'm not leaving without him."

The queen looked startled, though it was hard to

tell emotions on a dragonfly. "And if he chooses to stay?"

"He won't."

"It *is* his choice. If you stay, you might lose yourself waiting for him."

James grimaced, which was difficult, because his face was mostly numb. "Don't pretend to be concerned," he snapped. "If you really wanted to help, you'd stop making this accursed storm so I could find him without freezing to death."

The queen's laughter was a terrible, discordant clanging that set his teeth on edge. "Oh, James," she said. "It's *his* storm."

James opened his mouth, then shut it.

"I see," he said at length. "I should have known."

He felt blank. He'd truly thought it was Neverland or the fae or some other malicious force of nature trying to wash him into the sea, trying to keep him away from Peter.

But it had been *Peter*—Peter trying to keep him away, or just raging against the world, thoughtless of what he might be doing to James.

"Haven't you ever noticed that the sun comes out when he smiles?" the queen said. "It's another thing he wished for when he was a boy."

James laughed raggedly. "And all I wished for was a pirate crew."

"He is a far bolder storyteller than you."

"I can't leave him."

"How long do you think you can hold on to your memories?" the queen asked. "You'll forget. The temptation was always too much for you." She landed in his hands; they were suddenly warm, as though they had never been cold, and the gashes left on them by the rocky cliffs began to knit closed. James told himself it would be pointless, and probably deadly, to try to crush her. "You should go now," she said, "while you still can."

The idea of leaving without Peter tore at him. But so did the idea of being lost again, wandering in search of Peter until he forgot why he was searching, never returning to the life he had already come so close to losing.

"There's so much I wanted to tell him," James said quietly. "He ran off before I could say half of it."

The queen gave a little sigh and rose into the air, leaving behind a pool of silver dust. "Then say it," she said. "Surely you can think of a way."

~~*

On his way down the mountain, it started to snow.

Sixteen

The window was closed. Peter landed on the sill outside, balancing on his toes as the wind pushed him from side to side. The lacy white curtains were drawn shut, but he could see through them to the three beds in the nursery. His brothers were sleeping; they were lumps beneath under the covers.

"I'd better knock," Peter said. "What if they think I'm a burglar trying to break in?"

"Don't knock," Tink shimmered back. "You'll scare them." She leapt from his shoulder and spun a thread of silver into the crack between the shutters, pulling the latch up. The window came open, and Peter tiptoed down to the nursery floor.

Michael was snuffling in his sleep. Peter's heart swelled. He'd used to hate Michael's snoring, but that was before he'd thought he would never hear it again.

"Peter." Tink sounded anxious. Her fur ruffled his cheek. "This is goodbye," she said. "Are you sure?"

Peter nodded. "I'll miss you, Tink."

She flew up and kissed him on the brow, tickling him with her feelers. He almost laughed, but he couldn't quite. There was a funny feeling in his stomach, like he was going to be sick; he was happy and frightened all at once.

"Good luck," Tink said softly. "Wish for me if you need help again."

Peter nodded, and she left him with a sprinkle of fairy dust in his hair. He turned to watch her go through the window.

On the way back from Neverland, he and Tink had come up with a strategy for revealing his return to his brothers and parents. He'd be in bed when they woke, as if nothing had happened, and then insist on everyone gathering round in the parlor to hear the story of where he'd been.

But he tripped over a pile of blocks on his way back to bed, and with a gasp, John sat up and stared at him in the moonlight.

"Wendy?" he asked. His eyes were red. "Are you a ghost?"

"No," Peter said, startled by the idea. "And I'm not Wendy, I'm—"

"I saw you fly past the window," John said. He was using his most logical voice, but there was a tremble in it. "That's when I knew you must be dead."

"I'm not. I can fly." Peter tried to hop into the air to prove it, but came down hard on his heels. "The fairy dust must've worn off already—but I *could* fly. I went away to Neverland, but I decided to come back because I missed everyone. I missed *you*, John." John was looking at him like he had two heads, and Peter couldn't get it all out fast enough. "First, I've got to tell you something. My name's not Wendy anymore, it's Peter. Like Peter Pan, but Peter Darling. And you've got to start calling me your brother. I am, you see, but I didn't know I could be until I went away to Neverland—and then I just was a boy, and I knew I must have been all along."

He paused for breath, and John tilted his head to one side. "That," he said, "doesn't make any sense at all."

"I know it doesn't, but it's true. I can't explain it." Peter threw his arms wide, hoping John would see the difference in him, how free he felt. "It's a miracle."

John looked doubtful. Peter could see him running through this new information, trying to understand it. "You do look like a boy," he admitted. "But it's dress-up, isn't it?"

"*No*. It's for real."

John studied him. Then he leaned over and nudged Michael, who could sleep through anything, until he whimpered and began to stir. "Michael," he said, "Wendy's back, and she says she's a boy now."

"It's *Peter*," Peter protested, but he was cut off. Michael, half-asleep, sat up and saw a ragged stranger standing in his bedroom. He opened his mouth wide and gave an earsplitting scream. John and Peter clapped their hands over their ears, but even muffled, Peter heard his parents' footsteps pounding up the hall.

A moment later, the nursery door flew open.

Mr. and Mrs. Darling, too, screamed at the sight of Peter. Mrs. Darling flew forward and seized him in a bone-crushing hug, then pulled back in horror to stare at the mud on his face and leaves in his hair. "Dearest, who did it?" she asked. "Who took you? How did you escape?"

"Nobody took me," Peter protested. He squirmed his way out of the hug, chipping a bit of dirt off his cheek with one finger. "I went to Neverland."

"And she says her name's Peter now," John put in.

"You ought to say *his* name," Peter added. "As I'm a boy."

There was a tense silence. Then Mr. Darling,

standing above his wife and child, asked, "You went where?"

"Neverland," Peter said. "Like in the stories."

He drew a deep breath, preparing to launch into his full explanation again, but before he could speak Mr. Darling swept forward and seized him by the shoulders.

"*Do you have any idea what you've done*?" he bellowed, his face red. His fingers squeezed at Peter's shoulders like he meant to crush them. "We thought you were abducted! Killed! Locked up somewhere by some degenerate who kidnaps little girls from their beds! We've had police crawling over half of London for a *month*! Your brothers thought they'd never see their sister again!" He punctuated each roar with a shake of Peter's shoulders. Peter had never seen his father so angry; all he could do was shake in his grip. "And now," George Darling snarled, "you're back to say you *ran away*? You thought ruining your family's happiness was one of your little nursery games?"

"I'm sorry!" Peter burst out, tears filling his eyes. "I didn't know what to do! I didn't think you'd be upset—"

"Oh, *Wendy*," Mrs. Darling said. She was weeping. "How could you think that? How could you do this?"

"It's a disgrace," Mr. Darling snapped. "*Better* that she'd been kidnapped. Explaining to everyone we know—and the police to boot—that she ran away and came back looking like something that crawled out of the sewer—"

Mrs. Darling clapped her hands over her mouth, tears streaming over her fingers. "They can't know, George."

"I'm back now!" Peter shouted, desperately trying to be heard. John and Michael were watching in stunned silence, flattened back against their pillows by the force of their father's anger. "I came back! I came back because I love you, and John, and Michael—" He could barely speak through the lump in his throat. "I thought you'd be happy to see me!"

"I'd have been happy years ago," Mr. Darling said, "if you'd have grown up and started acting like a responsible young woman with a single thought in her head. *Neverland*." He spat the name. "I'd like to know where you've really been, and how on earth you've been conducting yourself for the last month."

"I've been in *Neverland*!" Peter tore himself out of his father's hands and backed toward the window. "John knows! He saw me fly up to the window."

Everyone turned to John, who fidgeted nervously with his blanket. "I did see something odd," he said. "I thought it was a ghost, but..."

"I will not have her dragging her brothers into her delusions," Mr. Darling ground out.

"It's true!" Peter yelled. He was getting angry. "I'll prove it to you! Tink!" He spun around and sprinted toward the window seat. "Tink, I need your help—"

Mrs. Darling screamed. "George, what if she jumps?"

Before he could reach it, Peter's father lunged forward and swept him over his shoulder, carrying him from the nursery. Peter pummeled his father's back with his fists, but Mr. Darling's grip was like iron.

They locked him in the washroom down the hall from the nursery. Peter cried and kicked fruitlessly at the door for a while, but when he exhausted himself, pressed up against instead to listen to his parents talking.

"Something must have happened," Mrs. Darling

was saying, low and anguished. "Someone must've done something to her. The boys aren't disturbed the way she is."

"Maybe, Mary. Maybe. I was against letting her room with the boys, you remember?"

"Don't start blaming me, George, please. I can't stand it right now. She loved them, and she wanted to stay with them." Even bruised and shut in the washroom, Peter felt a stab of guilt at the sound of tears in his mother's voice. "There must be something we can do to help her."

"I've heard of doctors who specialize in fixing people with... these kinds of problems," George grunted. "I'll call around in the morning. In the meantime, the boys must know not to say anything. And we'll keep her away from them. The last thing we need is another sick child."

Peter backed away from the door, his heart frozen.

He couldn't be separated from his brothers—half the reason he had come back at all was to be with John and Michael. He scrambled to the sink and started the water running, soaping up his muddy hands.

When his mother came to the door, his face and hands were clean, his hair brushed as best he could brush it and picked free of leaves. The moment the door came open, he jumped forward and said, "I'm sorry for making you worry, mama. It was just a game."

Mary Darling's mouth fell open and she glanced at her husband.

"You don't need to send me to a doctor," Peter continued, in a rush. "And don't keep me away from John and Michael. I'll be good. I was just playing." He didn't have to exaggerate his tears; they came thick and overwhelming, choking him as he tried to get everything out. "I didn't mean to scare everyone. I'm Wendy, okay?"

"And what was all that about Neverland?" Mr. Darling said, dangerously calm. "About fairies and pirates and magic and things?"

"There's no such thing," Peter said, and squeezed his eyes shut.

~~*

He felt the cold before he was fully awake, shivers chasing him out of his dreams.

Peter uncurled stiffly from the position he'd slept in, huddled against a heap of Red Dog's old clothes and a mountain of gold coins. He hadn't closed the door to the treasure room; through it, he saw the lakeshore blanketed in snow, the waterfall turned to a monument of ice.

He'd been halfway hoping James would wake him up, having decided to stay with him; he'd thought, of all the places, this might be the one James would come to. He'd thought that, of all things, James might come back for his spider silk coat.

Peter didn't know how long he'd been asleep, but by the looks of the world outside, certainly long enough for James to leave Neverland. So James was gone. He was alone.

Peter rubbed his hands together against the cold, shuddering and willing himself not to cry. It was exactly as it had been ten years ago. He'd realized as a boy that Neverland was empty, that the Lost Boys who so resembled his brothers weren't really John and Michael, and then he'd known it wasn't worth it to stay. What was the point of being himself if he had to be alone?

He picked himself up and wandered out into the snow, wrapping his arms around himself. He remembered being wrapped up in James's coat, and bowed his head miserably, trying to remember the way it had smelled. It was the opposite of what he should have been doing, which was trying to forget.

If he could forget, he could find something worth having in this world. Otherwise, there would be no point in living at all.

Seventeen

The sea had turned to deep-green glass, stiff waves of ice rolling over the surface, cresting into icicles. Peter blew over it all on the bitter wind, finding Neverland white and soft beneath heavy snowdrifts. It was terribly quiet. The forest and mountains and hills and bays were all blanketed in frost, and their personalities were changed by it, warped into another world where the island was unmoving and stoic.

Mermaid Lagoon had frozen over, and Peter was afraid the merfolk had died or been trapped beneath the ice. But he found them sheltering inside a nearby cave, where the Lost Boys had lit a bonfire large enough to melt the ice.

They shrank from Peter as he flew in, staring at him like strangers. They were all present, except for Ernest.

"Where is he?" Peter asked.

"He left," Curly said tonelessly. "He said he was going home. It's Hook's fault. He came and told Ernest that we weren't real."

Peter stared at him, distantly hurt that James had taken something else from him, distantly horrified that he had never realized how much Curly resembled Michael.

Slightly, he thought, Slightly had looked just like John.

"Where did they go?" he asked.

"Ernest went down the shore," Curly said. "Hook

183

didn't say where he was going."

~~*

Ernest couldn't have been gone long. His footprints were still visible in the beach, sunk deep and icy in the snow. He had gone off in a strange direction, circling around the cliffs where the shore was narrow and the sea pressed up against it. The cliffs had come down intermittently in the storm, leaving the beach divided between landslides of frozen mud. Peter flew above them, afraid he was going to see the trail of Ernest's footprints end beneath one of the collapsed cliffs.

But when he finally saw Ernest, he was sitting on a log with his wounded leg stretched out, staring at a particularly large section of cliff that had fallen and blocked his path.

Peter landed quietly beside him. He was still trying to think of something to say when Ernest glanced over, saw him, and yelped in alarm. He fell off the log, or would have if Peter hadn't jumped forward to steady him.

"*Peter*!" Ernest flushed as he said his name. "You're okay!" Before Peter could reply, he wrapped his arms around Peter's neck, pulling him into a bone-squeezing hug. Peter, startled, patted tentatively at his back and laughed a little. The hug went on for a long time—Ernest didn't seem to want to let go, and Peter allowed it, grateful to see him alive.

"Of course I'm okay," he said, when Ernest finally released him. "You didn't think I'd let the pirates get the better of me, did you?"

"Never," Ernest said, and broke into a smile. There

were snowflakes clinging to his pale hair, his round eyes made gray by the sky reflecting on the glass sea. "Where have you been?"

"Nowhere," Peter said. "Where are you going?"

Ernest's expression changed. Peter saw him remembering, strengthening his resolve. "Home," he said.

"I thought your family made you unhappy," Peter said. "I thought they were trying to fix something that wasn't wrong with you."

Ernest nodded. He looked down. "All of that was true," he said. "But I still love them. And I still want to *live*. Even if I have to go home and run away for real. I'm a grown man now. I could make it on my own." A small smile crossed his lips. "Maybe my parents missed me so much they won't mind if I'm not fixed."

"I'm happy for you," Peter said. He was, even though he felt empty of the hope that filled Ernest's eyes. *Don't leave me too*, he wanted to say, but it wouldn't be fair. It wouldn't make up for losing James, either. "You're right. You should go home. How do you get there?"

"There was always a corner in my room I walked into," Ernest said. "Around the fireplace—the edge of it looked like a cliff in silhouette. I'd step around it and the rug would turn into beach sand, and I'd walk across the rocks under the cliff, and then I'd finally see mermaids in the distance and know I was here." He gestured at the collapsed bluff that had blocked him. "It's on the other side of all this."

"I'll help you," Peter said. "Give me your hand."

Ernest did so, and Peter wrapped an arm around his waist, pretending not to notice the color that seeped into Ernest's cheeks. He kicked off and carried them both in a long arc over the fallen cliff, and then set Ernest down in the sand on the other side.

"There," Ernest exclaimed, pointing. The beach turned suddenly inland, leaving a rocky outcrop of cliff in silhouette, past which the forest was invisible. "See? It looks like my fireplace. I'll go around that corner and be home." He took a deep breath, turning to Peter and taking him by the arms. "Are you sure you'll be all right?"

"I'm always all right," Peter said, and knew it sounded like a lie. "I'll be fine."

"Maybe we'll meet again someday," Ernest said, and pulled Peter into another tight embrace. This time, when he let go, he turned quickly and didn't look back. He walked around the corner of the cliff and he was gone.

Peter didn't bother checking to see if he could follow, if he could watch Ernest vanish. He knew it would only make him feel more alone, and he already felt silent inside, muffled like the snow falling on the sand.

~~*

There was a flower growing in the place where Tink had died, poking up through the snow, a golden bud closed tight. Peter hunched over in the snow beside it, ignoring the damp soaking into his trousers. He stroked one of the petals.

He felt, as if in answer, a faint hum of magic from inside it. "Tink?" he asked.

"Not quite," the queen said.

Peter twisted around to see her floating down from a nearby tree. She landed on the bud, glistening in the bright reflections from the snow. "The fae are a part of Neverland," she said. "We return to the earth when we die, and something new grows from our ashes."

"Did I make that up?"

"Not everything is your truth," she said tersely. "Some things are just true."

Peter frowned, bundling his arms around himself.

"So," the queen said. "Are you to join us, Pan? You wouldn't be alone. Other dreamers have chosen to stay, and in time, the things that plague the human mind do cease to trouble you."

That was exactly what he wanted—or so he would have thought, before James. Now it sounded as hollow as everything else. "You can't really make it go away," he said bitterly. "Nothing here means anything."

"No?" Her eyes glittered at him. "Did it mean nothing to you to discover what it felt like to be surrounded by playmates who treated you as a boy? Do you regret learning what it felt like to fall in love with a man?"

"And now what?" Peter snapped. "I lost my family. I lost James, and Tink, and Ernest, and everyone. I don't want to be here. I don't want to be alone. What good was it to find out who I am and what I want if I had to be *alone*?"

The queen studied him for a moment longer. Then she fluttered into the air, wings chiming. "Come with me," she said.

She flew away, a warm light that cut through the snow. Peter almost didn't follow; he didn't want to see any more of her. But there was nothing else to do, and she was the only other living thing in sight, so he hauled himself to his feet and took off after her.

They flew high over Neverland, up to the mountain he and Ernest had climbed to find the fairy commune. They came down in the clearing beneath the dead commune tree, which was heaped with fresh snow. The queen landed in the crook of two tree branches, where the boughs had created a small shelter from the damp.

A little scroll was tucked into the wood, covered in silver dust that seemed to be repelling the snow.

"It's for you," the queen said. "Read it."

Peter reached up apprehensively and took the scroll, unrolling it. His heart jumped at the sight of the handwriting; it was Captain Hook's, but scratchier and less elegant. Peter sank down in the snow, gripping the letter in both hands.

It read:

Dear Peter,

I'd write you a novel, but you're freezing me to death, so I haven't much time.

I'd like to think I understand why you ran away, because I did the same thing. I loved a man who died in the war after I'd staked all my hopes for happiness on him. I was desperately lonely. I came back to Neverland because I couldn't imagine anything happier than this place, and I lost myself here. However your family treated you, it must have hurt as much as I was hurting then. I'm sorry. I don't know what my sympathy means to you, but you have it. I hate to think of you being unhappy. If I could, I'd do everything in my power to make you happy again.

I suppose there's no point in being coy in a letter like this. I adore you. I adore your stories. I want a chance to adore you in the real world, whoever we are out there, if you'll let me. I don't want you to stay here, not only because I care about you, but because you've saved my life, whether you like it or not—and I can't bear the thought of running away while you stay trapped. Actually, I'm being selfish. I want to be with you. I want you to come with me, and I swear to God if you do, I'll give you whatever home I have left out there.

I've always come to Neverland by sea, from north of Pelican Island. If you go that way, and sail on into the horizon, you'll see England to the left of the sun. Go straight toward it, and you ought to come to a cottage by the river. I hope to be there waiting for you.

Please pull your head out of your ass and come find me. I have quite a lot of rebuilding to do, and I'd like to do it with you.

So—all my love,
James

P.S. I've just remembered my surname. It's Harrington. That's one more thing I wouldn't have gotten back without your help.

Please, please come.

Peter looked up. His heart was thundering in his ears. "When did he leave this?" he demanded. "How long has it been? Where is he?"

"You read the letter." The queen spread her wings, showering him in dust. "Go north, Pan."

Peter shot up in the air, streaking toward the island's northmost tip. The snow was so thick it was almost impossible to see where beach ended and sea began; thick snowdrifts covered both, blowing in the wind.

He didn't know what it meant to leave Neverland by a different route. The path between the stars that led from Neverland to the Darling house was complex; Peter had only made it before with Tink's help. He didn't know if he could fly out of Neverland and find his way to someone else's home. He could easily imagine himself getting lost somewhere in the night.

But a chance of getting lost, he decided, was better than the certainty of losing James.

The whole island lay below him soon as he climbed into the sky, gray clouds above and silver-white canopy below, a blank page where there should have been a map. It was easy to leave behind when he could see how formless it had become. Out past the northern tip of the island he flew, toward the odd little Pelican Island where he and the Lost Boys had once discovered trees covered in sweet berries guarded by crocodiles and tigers. It was as buried in snow as the rest of Neverland. Beyond it, the sea spread into the horizon, growing bluer and brighter as the ice thinned.

Peter had never sailed out this far. He could only wonder what was ahead.

But before the ice ended—when it was still quite thick—Peter looked down to see something stuck in the frost. He dipped lower, and there it was.

A very small boat.

The dinghy was caught in frozen waves, its prow lifted out from water by frost that had formed beneath it. Inside the boat was a man who must have spent several days sitting at that uncomfortable angle, far from shore and tauntingly close to the edge of the ice sheet.

Peter slowed as he approached the boat, afraid he was mistaken in thinking he knew the color of the man's waistcoat. But then he saw the hook jutting from James's sleeve, and the feeling that broke open in his chest was like spring coming in a single moment. Relief made him feel so light it was a struggle to descend; he came down like a dandelion clock on the end of the boat.

James was hunched over, carpeted in frost, snow heaped on his shoulders. He gave a stiff, startled jolt when Peter landed before him, wrenching his head up as if it had been frozen in place. There was ice in his beard.

"James!" Peter dropped to his knees and grabbing James's gaunt, bloodless hand. He gasped at how cold it was, clutching it until it began to leech the heat from his own skin. "You're *freezing*."

"Peter?" James asked hoarsely. He looked calm, but his tone betrayed him. His teeth chattered when he tried to speak. "And h-here I thought I'd been destined to spend the rest of my life in this b-bloody ice sheet."

"I'm sorry," Peter said. "It's my fault. I made a mess of Neverland."

James gave a weak chuckle. "How t-typical." Peter reached up and laid a hand across his cheek, his fingertips melting the frost. James stared at him with wondering, sky-blue eyes. "And to w-what," he managed, "do I owe the honor?"

"I got your letter." Peter smiled tentatively, and watched a slow smile spread across James's face as well.

"*And?*"

Peter felt the words in his mouth, tasted their sweetness and let them linger there before he said, "I adore you too."

There was a crack from beneath him as the ice broke under the prow and the dinghy lurched downward, plunging its keel back into the meltwater. James shot forward, arms flung out to catch himself, but Peter caught him first.

They fell in the bottom of the boat with their arms around each other, sudden heat enveloping them as the sun broke through the clouds and spilled light over them. James was flushed, astonished; his mouth was slightly open when Peter kissed it, and then his hand was in Peter's hair, clutching it tight as he pressed their bodies together.

The boat rocked and swayed as the ice sheet split apart, but Peter hardly felt it.

~~*

"You are extraordinarily dramatic," James said, "and no one should ever have given you power over the weather."

They were sitting in the dinghy amid an ocean of broken, glittering ice floes that were drifting gradually further and further apart. The sun, which had come out so suddenly, had stayed and was beginning to sink down toward the horizon. In the distance, Neverland was melting, new waterfalls pouring into the sea, the water shining orange in the sunset.

"It's not so bad now," Peter said. "Anyway, I wasn't doing it on purpose."

"In all fairness, if it had been me, I'd have made a blizzard too." James kissed him, his beard scratching at Peter's cheeks. "And in all fairness, I find that dramatic streak of yours very charming."

His hand was perfectly warm now, but Peter couldn't stop holding it.

"I have quite a nice house," James added. "At least I hope I still do. It's out in the forest—I've always kept to myself. I think you'd like it."

"It sounds perfect," Peter said. He shut his eyes and felt the question James was about to ask. "I do want to come with you. I'm just afraid I'll wake up and be back with my family instead of with you."

James's fingers drifted, tucked a strand of hair behind Peter's ear. "I won't let go until you're safely at my door. If the wind tries to snatch you up, it'll have to take me too, and we'll fight our way out together. How about that?"

Peter took a deep breath and gathered the scent of Neverland in his lungs, the feeling of himself, the boy he had discovered all those years ago. It steadied him. Ten years hadn't managed to take him away from himself; nothing could.

And James would be with him, holding him close.

"All right," he said.

James wrapped an arm firmly around Peter's waist and took a grip on the leftmost oar. "Shall we try it, then?" he asked. "Shall we see how we end up?"

"Yes," Peter said, and took up the other oar.

Eighteen

The wind came in through the window and ruffled Peter's hair.

The breeze had an unfamiliar smell, earthy and slightly boggy, tinged with the scent of dandelions and other early flowers. It was the smell that alerted Peter to being somewhere different, somewhere entirely new, so that he opened his eyes.

He was curled on a window seat, curtains billowing gently above his head. His head was resting on a broad arm, his back pressed to a broad chest, and he could hear ducks quacking outside. It was remarkably quiet, and he realized why—there were no city sounds, no grumbling cars, no people chattering. This wasn't London.

Peter sat up slowly and looked outside. Through the window, which was set in a frame painted with blue flowers, Peter could see the banks of a river. A flurry of ducks were bickering as they floated by, sunlight flashing on their feathers. The water was calm and wide, and a narrow dock jutted out over it. A small boat was tied at the dock.

When he forced himself to remember—and it was like remembering part of a dream—he knew that he had been sitting in that boat when James rowed it down the stream. Much like the window of the Darling house, this stream became something else at night, flowing beyond its banks so a little boy in a boat could find his way to the seas of Neverland.

And find his way back.

The body behind him stirred and an arm came to curl around his waist. Peter startled at the warmth and intimacy of that movement, at the familiar voice that murmured, "Peter?"

Peter turned around, folding his arms over his chest self-consciously.

It was unmistakably James. His hair was still a vast lion's mane, though perhaps less from purposeful style than from having gone many years uncut. His nose was still big and hawkish, but without the piratical leer, it just made him look a little awkward, like most birds do. He wore a silky dressing gown patterned with red and gold diamonds, every bit as ridiculous as what he had worn as captain of the *Jolly Roger*.

His eyes were the same: soft, blue, and arresting. He reached up and stroked Peter's cheek with the backs of his fingers, traced his thumb along the curve of his jaw, and must have felt Peter flush beneath his touch.

"My God," he said, wondering. "It is you." His real voice was carefully measured, quieter.

Peter nodded, his words caught in his throat, a thousand questions on his tongue. He ran a tentative hand up James's chest, through the silky folds of his dressing gown, and felt his heart beat, quick and nervous, against his fingertips. They were both afraid, he thought, both exposed to each other. Both present, unkempt, and—real.

Knowing Hook made it obvious, instantly, how he was to James exactly what Pan was to Peter. Someone bolder, more fantastical, less frightened, less lonely. A dream of someone he could be in a different world.

But James was an ordinary man who liked the same ridiculous clothes, and in his face Peter could see all the caution and temperance he must have thrown aside to be a pirate king. He was perfect. Peter curled his fingers in silk, his heart pounding, dizzy with love and fear.

He didn't know what James was seeing as he studied Peter in silence, equally wide-eyed. Then James smiled—a slow, helpless, affectionate smile—and Peter grinned back. Tears sprang into his eyes and he let go of James's dressing gown to wipe them away, embarrassed and absurdly happy.

James cleared his throat and ran a comforting hand down his side. He sat up, his leg pressing to Peter's hip, and reached for a pair of round spectacles resting on the table nearby.

And sneezed. That small movement had disturbed such a cloud of dust as to envelop them for a moment. Peter scrambled up and stuck his head out the window, coughing; James joined him on the windowsill, wiping many years of dust from his glasses. "Oh dear," he managed, between sneezes. "I suppose no one—kept up with the housekeeping. I've—brought you back to a bit of a wasteland."

"That's all right," Peter said. His own voice startled him; it was higher than it had been, more refined.

James settled his glasses on his nose, smiling. The spectacles gave him an anxious look.

He still had only one hand; his other arm ended at the wrist. He caught Peter's curious look. "As a boy," he said ruefully, "it was more exciting to imagine a hook than a heavy prosthetic."

"So I really wasn't the one who cut off your hand."

"Not unless you were in some kind of conspiracy

with my mother's womb," James said, and Peter laughed.

Peter realized he was waiting for some kind of probing curiosity in return—some remark on what Peter sounded like, or worse on his body—but James's only encroachment on the subject was to say, "Your shirt has seen better days. Would you like one of mine? Assuming all my clothes haven't been eaten by moths."

All at once it became easier to breathe. "Yes," Peter said. "Please."

"Don't tell me you have manners in this world," James said dryly. "I'll die of shock."

~~*

While James set off to investigate what had become of his wardrobe, a handkerchief tied over his nose and mouth, Peter went around yanking open all the windows and doors to let in light and air. He did it from outside, evading the worst of the dust. James's cottage had been halfway reclaimed by nature; it was small enough to vanish amongst the nearby trees, and little plants had taken up residence in nooks and crannies along the walls. There were birds nesting on the roof, and they squawked at Peter like he was an invader in their territory. It was a true fairytale house.

The interior was a different story. It was shrouded in such thick dust that it was difficult to tell the character of the house at all. Peter pulled his shirt up over his nose and went wandering through the dusky parlor, running his fingers through the dust to uncover the colors underneath. The house was cluttered in a way that didn't surprise Peter after seeing how James kept his quarters aboard the *Jolly Roger*. Much like the captain's cabin, the cottage had treasure piled everywhere, waiting to be unearthed—except instead of gold and jewels, it was paintings.

There were landscapes and nudes, dreamy abstracts and vivid sunsets. James painted in exquisite detail and piercing color. On the wall, dulled by the dust motes floating through the air, there was an enormous canvas depicting the *Jolly Roger* at anchor. The ship was bathed in the glittering of the sun on the water, and Peter felt sure that he had seen it look just like this. He traced his fingers carefully along the black rigging, feeling the ridges and waves of dry paint.

It shouldn't have surprised him to discover the kind of artist James was—all his eye for scene-setting and detail flowed obviously onto the canvas. The beauty of it still stunned him; it was a whole new dimension of James he hadn't known before.

He found his way to the kitchen next, which looked out on a garden overgrown with wildflowers. What food there was had long ago spoiled, and Peter grimaced when he glanced in the cupboards. The stone floor was freezing beneath his toes; the hearth clearly hadn't seen use in a long time. He found an old box of matches next to a pile of logs and managed to get a fire going.

He jumped when James spoke behind him. "I was going to offer to make you breakfast, but I realize that may be a lost cause."

Peter straightened up and James held out a dusty bundle of clothing for him. "It's probably a bit large," he said apologetically, "but for the moment..."

"I don't care," Peter said. "Thank you."

~~*

The trousers were miles too long, even when Peter cuffed the legs. The socks bagged in the ankles, and the shirt and sweater were equally large. But when Peter finally managed to get the collars to lie right and glanced at the reflection he'd carved out of the dust on James's mirror, a shock went through him.

This was the face which had haunted him all his life, the one he had looked in the eye on the day he left the Darling house for the last time. The hair, messy and short, enthusiastically curling without the weight of his old braid to drag it down. The stubborn chin. The clear, sharp, sullen eyes full of everything he had never been allowed to be.

Peter ran his hands over himself slowly, breathing tentatively, feeling the weight of his chest under his shirt. He had given this body up. He had thought it belonged to Wendy, to the girl he wasn't. He had let his family make him believe that the only way he would ever be a boy was to be born again in a different shape, leaving everything of his body and history behind.

He breathed out and settled in the feeling of being himself, of being something whole.

It was a long time before he went back to find James puttering in the kitchen, looking overwhelmed by the state of the house. He still had a smile for Peter when he saw him in the doorway, however. He said, "There you are."

Peter spread his arms and gave a bow like the one the fairies had taught him. "Here I am."

"I swear if you weren't here I'd go running straight back to Neverland from all this mess." James's face took on a fretful look as Peter came to join him by the rusted stove. "And frankly, I wouldn't blame you if you felt cheated—here I promised you a home, and I never mentioned it was a home for all the world's mice and spiders as well. Or that there wouldn't be anything to eat. Or that I hadn't even put away my easels before I ran off to live the rest of my life in a dream—"

"We'll have to go foraging," Peter said. "I saw some edible wildflowers in your yard. I'm almost sure the mushrooms by the river aren't poisonous."

James paused with his mouth open, then shut it and cleared his throat, looking as if he were trying very hard not to smile. "Alternately," he said, "there's a town a few miles away where we could buy bacon and eggs."

"Come now, Captain," Peter said. "That's hardly the spirit of the thing."

The corner of James's mouth twitched. "You're not going to get me to eat wild mushrooms that easily in this world, I warn you. But now that you mention it, there is an apple tree down the river, or at least there used to be. That ought to be safe."

Peter bumped against his side. "Let's start there."

~~*

They followed a path that meandered between sunlight and the green-gold shade of birch trees, all of it damp with dew. Peter wore a pair of James's boots, laced tight to make up for how large they were on his feet. It was quiet except for sweet birdsong and the stream trickling by. James pointed out the locations of several of his paintings along the river as they walked. Peter could remember finding places like this in

Neverland; he thought he had sat by this very stream as a child, running his toes through the water, and wondered if they had been sharing dreams with each other all along.

That was one of many questions he left unasked. There was too much to say, so neither of them said anything for a while.

"This is very strange," James said, breaking the silence. "I don't know what I'm going to say to anyone who asks where you came from—or where I've been, for that matter."

"Say you've been traveling the world to find inspiration for your paintings," Peter said. "Say I'm a model you discovered and had to bring home with you."

"My own Dorian Gray," James said with a laugh. "No—you're far more than a model, don't you think?"

"I'm not sure," Peter said. "I don't know what I'm going to do." He felt his way through the uncertainty. "I always thought the only way to grow up was to be… her. I don't know what to do as me."

James's brow wrinkled as he thought. Then he said, "I have a typewriter in the attic. We could dust it off if you'd like to keep telling stories."

Peter startled. "You mean write books?"

"Or plays, or poetry—whatever suits you."

Peter's skin prickled at the very idea, like a bolt of lightning had run through him. "Yes," he said. His voice cracked when he realized James had cut easily to the heart of him. "I'd like that."

James smiled.

They came to the apple tree around the next bend in the path. The tree had an unusual shape, taller and more withholding than the average apple, with what little fruit there was clustered toward the upper branches. The apples were small and green. James sighed. "I always thought the appeal of apple trees was that you could grab something to eat as you walked by. This one you have to shake and pray that the fruit falls—Peter, what are you doing?"

Peter finished kicking off his overlarge boots and socks and rucked his trousers up to his knees. "How many apples do you want?"

"Are you going to break your ankle on your first day back in the world? You do remember you can't actually fly?"

Peter grinned at him. "That's half the challenge," he said, and scrambled up the tree. It didn't go quite as smoothly as he'd hoped it would. He was used to the way things worked in Neverland, where he was as strong as he wanted to be and found branches conveniently located wherever he reached for them. Here, his arms were shaking by the time he managed to haul himself up to a split in the branches and rest. Glancing down made him dizzy, even though he was only a few meters from the ground.

"I hope by this point you've realized that I live out in the woods alone," James called, in an anxious tone poorly disguised as chastisement. "If you fall and hurt yourself, there's no fairy dust to fix you."

Peter tested the strength of the next branch. "I won't hurt myself," he called back, dragging himself up to the next intersection and stretching a hand toward the nearest apple. "I'm the spirit of youth and joy, remember?"

"You're a grown man and a nuisance."

"I'm your nuisance," Peter said, and then paused, embarrassed with himself and glad that he was too high up for James to see it. James fell into an equally awkward silence until Peter began tossing crabapples at him.

When he had thrown down what seemed like plenty of fruit for the two of them, Peter began an incautious descent, sliding down through the branches and scraping his palms on the rough bark. He misjudged the height of the last drop and hit the ground a little hard, tripping into James, who dropped an armful of apples to catch him.

"Thanks," Peter said, grinning.

James's cheeks were flushed, and he looked a funny combination of annoyed and charmed, scowling even as his mouth curved into a smile. He had wrapped his arm around Peter's waist; he straightened Peter up, setting him back on his feet. He stopped drawing away when Peter caught the front of his shirt in his fingers.

His mouth was softer in this world, absent the tang of rum and salt, but something of the ocean still swept over Peter when they kissed.

Fin

About the Author

Austin Chant is a bitter millennial, decent chef, and a queer, trans writer of romance and speculative fiction. He cohosts the Hopeless Romantic, a podcast dedicated to exploring LGBTQIA+ love stories and the art of writing romance. He currently lives in Seattle, in a household of wildly creative freelancers who all spend too much time playing video games. Website: austinchant.com